Mary Hallock Foote

John Bodewin's Testimory

Mary Hallock Foote

John Bodewin's Testimory

ISBN/EAN: 9783337398668

Printed in Europe, USA, Canada, Australia, Japan

Cover: Foto ©Andreas Hilbeck / pixelio.de

More available books at **www.hansebooks.com**

JOHN BODEWIN'S TESTIMONY

BY

MARY HALLOCK FOOTE

AUTHOR OF "THE LED-HORSE CLAIM," "FRIEND BARTON'S
CONCERN," ETC.

BOSTON

TICKNOR AND COMPANY

1886

CONTENT

JOHN BODEWIN'S TESTIMONY.

CHAPTER I.

IN THE BURNT WOODS.

THE western slope of the Park range, as it sinks into the valley of the Arkansas, is clothed to the timber-line with monotonous forests of pine and fir. In winter this dark zone of trees looks darker for the zone of snows above it; in spring the patches of sunlight on the mountain-side bring out a paler and more vivid green; the lower gulches, lined with aspens, in autumn show a streak of faded gold; but at all seasons, from the highest of the mountain's lights to the deepest of its shadows, the range of color is slight.

The deepest shadow on the mountains is one which does not change with the seasons or pass with the clouds. It covers an area of many acres. Within its limits the trees are still standing, but leafless and blackened from root to crown. They are the unburied dead which the forest fires have left on the field after one of their wild forays. In the course of years the wind will flay them and the snows will bleach them to the grayish whiteness of old bones. But in the summer of 187–, when the Eagle Bird and Uinta lode claims were first discovered, the burnt woods which covered them had but just met their fate. Each separate tree was an effigy of desolation, uplifting its charred and rigid limbs as if in mute attestation of its wrongs. The wind could get no more music out of them; the few birds which nested so far above the valley forsook their branches; the traveller missed their spicy shade. They could no longer offer either rest, shelter, or concealment to any living creature. But their neighborhood was as good as any other for the location of a mine.

Colonel Harkins, the owner of the Eagle Bird and the Uinta, did not trouble himself about his environment. He looked about him and saw that the dead trees were fit for fuel, if not for building and the timbering of shafts. He saw that the slope of the hill was sufficient for drainage, and for the future ore-dumps of unknown value to lean their cone-shaped mounds against. He reckoned the cost of a wagon-road to the nearest camp, two miles away, which formed the nucleus of many lesser camps and outlying mines scattered far and near along the sides of the range or concealed in the folds of its forest garment.

An old hunter's and prospector's trail, starting in the valley, took its way deviously but always upwards in the direction of the pass. A short distance beyond the two claims it was joined by a trail from the camp. Thus the new mines, though lonely in their situation, were not inaccessible.

One afternoon, about four o'clock, a man came out of the Eagle Bird tunnel, extinguished his candle as its rays turned sickly in the daylight, and, mounting his horse, followed the trail which led onward into the forest. The sun stood nearly opposite across the valley, and he raised his hand to his hat-brim, as if blinded by the glare. He sat his horse easily, lounging a little forward after the manner of men who spend many hours in the saddle in solitary, uneventful journeyings. He was a youngish, slenderly made man, with a distinctly good bearing. Even as he jogged along on his bald-faced bay in the bleak untempered light, you felt that he was one whom life had refined and sobered, if it had not distinguished him with any great measure of joy or of success. His thin, smooth cheeks were darkly tanned ; the close-shorn, light-brown hair, without a trace of gold in it, showed by its difference of texture rather than color against his temples and neck. His hands were the slender, pointed hands which go with a supple, small-jointed frame. His beauty, what there was of it, consisted chiefly in this harmony of parts, uniting in a personality unique but singularly unaggressive. The rider's name was John Bodewin.

The trail, now turning away from the valley, gave him the benefit of his own shadow opposed to the sun. Its broad light streamed before him into the forest and shone full in the faces of two people at a little distance from him, who had turned at the sound of his horse's feet, — a middle-aged gentleman, seated in a rather disconsolate attitude on the smooth, barkless trunk of a fallen tree, and a young lady in a riding-habit, who stood near him and was speaking to him when Bodewin saw them first. The gentleman was of stout proportions and fresh complexion, intensified by a recent coat of sunburn. Bodewin recognized Mr. Newbold at once ; the dark-eyed girl beside him was presumably Mr. Newbold's daughter.

"Did you ever know anything so still as this place?" she had been saying. "I cannot hear a sound except that horse's tread. Some one is coming who is in no hurry, it seems."

A moment later Bodewin appeared at the turn of the trail.

"*He's* in no hurry," Mr. Newbold remarked sulkily, eyeing the horseman's approach, "if he takes his own business as coolly as he does other people's."

"Do you know him, papa?" the girl asked in surprise. Bodewin had welcomed the sight of a fair woman in the forest, and involuntarily paid it the homage of a more erect seat in his saddle, and a hasty restoration of his hat from the angle of comfort on a hot afternoon, with the sun on the back of one's neck, to the level of decorum under all circumstances. He passed the group at his horse's slowest walk.

"How d'you do, Bodewin? Still here, you see," Mr. Newbold said, touching his hat to him.

Bodewin made some civil though inaudible reply. He had a speaking acquaintance with Mr. Newbold, but he could hardly have been surprised to see him there or elsewhere, since that gentleman's system of movements was quite unknown to him.

Miss Newbold had been two weeks in the camp, and Bodewin had not sought to see her or be presented to her for reasons personal, referring to her father, and local, referring to the city of her father's adoption. He had a preconceived idea of what a Kansas City girl was likely to be. But who was he, John Bodewin, a native of one of the little Sound cities of Connecticut, that he should be setting up geographical standards and prejudging his countrywomen by them? And what was there about Newbold to make it incredible that he should be the father of a girl, too handsome not to be supposed to know it herself, who kept her quiet pose under the eyes of a stranger with an unconcern that had in it as little of bravado as of stolidity?

"So that is Mr. John Bodewin!" Miss Newbold said, with meditative emphasis.

"It's queer you should never have seen Bodewin!" her father remarked.

"I think I did see him once, without knowing it was he, coming out of the Wiltsie House with Mr. Craig."

"Where were you?"

"I was looking out of our window, papa, hoping every next man on the street would be you.

It was nearly eight o'clock, and I was simply perishing for my dinner."

"I suppose I must have come along after a while, as you didn't perish," said Mr. Newbold. "When was it you were so near dissolution ?"

"It was on Saturday, the nineteenth of June. I remember the date, because that morning you first told me about the lawsuit, and the text on my calendar was 'Keep o' the windy side of the law' — 'especially mining law,' I wrote underneath, and pinned it in the frame of your looking-glass. But you did not see it, because that afternoon our rooms were changed."

"You and Bodewin must consult the same oracle," said Mr. Newbold. "It was on that afternoon in Craig's office he positively refused to go on the case."

"Did he give you his reasons for declining, papa, or don't they give reasons ? "

" They do as they choose, generally. Bodewin choose to keep his to himself."

"I suppose he thinks we are quite in the wrong, and is too polite to say so."

" What he thinks is not precisely what we are after." Mr. Newbold moved restlessly and felt in his pockets for a handkerchief with which he removed the marks of charred pine-wood from his fingers. "He is supposed to have in his possession the facts we need to complete our case. If he would consent to part with them on the witness-stand, he might keep his opinion and welcome."

"Are these facts Mr. Bodewin's property exclusively, papa?"

"So far as I know, they are."

"Why, how wretched of him! He might as well be a Uinta man and done with it! Is he, do you suppose?"

"I don't profess to know, my dear, what he is!"

"Would any other person who happened to have the facts Mr. Bodewin has be as desirable a witness as he?"

"More so, perhaps. I have told you it is not Bodewin we want, but his facts. He is an expert, but in this case he is not asked to give an expert's testimony."

"What does it imply, do you think?"

"What does what imply?" Mr. Newbold took his cross-examination with a half-bored, half-amused smile. He had a sharp eye, in a mild, blunt-featured, smooth-shaven face.

"His refusing to testify, papa," his daughter patiently explained.

"It might imply, among other things, that Mr. Bodewin is not in want of money at present."

"Are witnesses paid much money for their testimony?"

"Depends on the witness, and the nature of the testimony, and on what you call much."

"Papa, you will have to hold me! You look so comfortable, and there is nowhere else to sit." Miss Newbold pushed aside her father's cane and seated herself, with a smile half deprecating, half playful, on his knee.

"If I look comfortable, my looks belie me," he sighed, adjusting himself to the weight of her slender figure. "Why *do* we sit? Why don't we move on?"

"Where shall we move to, if you please? Back to the Eagle Bird, and sit on the piazza with the sun in our eyes? *Look* at that valley!"

"Looks hot, don't it?"

"Papa, how — much — did you offer Mr. Bodewin?"

"How much what?" Mr. Newbold doggedly held out.

"Poor papa!" said his daughter, holding him

by the shoulders and laughing, with her face close to his. "It's no use pretending you are not going to tell me. You know you are; — it's only a question of time."

"Come, get up, Josephine! You're too heavy; this log needs a saddle on it."

"I never was too heavy before."

"You never before found me reduced to such a painful extremity for a seat."

"How much, papa? and I'll let you up."

"Let me up first, and then we'll see about it. What do you want to know for?"

"I want to know partly because you don't want to tell me. Come, papa! On compulsion, you know. A man may say anything under pressure. There's nothing yielding about you. Besides, it's only mines. It hasn't anything to do with your real business!"

Mr. Newbold relieved himself by a resolute push from the burden of his daughter's loveliness, and got himself stiffly upon his feet.

"By George, you *are* heavy!" he muttered reproachfully, as he limped a few steps along the trail.

"Now, papa, be a good boy. Be frank with me for once," Josephine pleaded, still laughing and dragging upon his arm with her hands locked within it. "You need never hope to look upon the Eagle Bird again unless you tell me how — much — money — you offered Mr. Bodewin."

"Well, to be frank with you," said Mr. Newbold, attempting to light a cigar under difficulties, "I never offered Mr. Bodewin a penny. But my lawyers offered him — five thousand dollars, and be hanged to him," he concluded, as he tossed his extinguished match into the dust. Josephine released his arm suddenly and confronted him in sober amazement.

"Papa, I wish I had some facts I could dispose of at that rate. Isn't that a good deal of money to offer a man for just telling the truth?"

"Would you expect a professional man to spend his time in court on another man's case for the witness-fees?" Mr. Newbold asked.

"How much of his time would he have to spend?"

"An hour, perhaps, actually on the stand." Mr. Newbold yielded the point carelessly.

"I should not have supposed, from Mr. Bodewin's appearance as he rode through the woods just now, that his time was worth five thousand dollars an hour."

"There are hours and hours of a man's time, my dear. This may not be one of Bodewin's five-thousand-dollar hours."

"Papa, you know perfectly well there is no man living who can earn five thousand dollars honestly in an hour."

"Do I?" said Mr. Newbold, unconcernedly. "I wish I knew by personal experience to the contrary."

"Well, I am glad he did not take it. I respect him for not taking it. At the same time —"

"You would like to know whether he was offered more by the other side to keep quiet."

They were walking now along the trail, Josephine preceding her father. As he spoke and laughed his easy, unmirthful laugh, she looked back at him. The level sunbeams striking across her eyes turned the blackness of their thick, curved lashes to a reddish brown.

"Papa, do you believe that?"

"I'm not a man of many beliefs," Mr. Newbold replied, with the manner of one who is done with a subject.

Josephine wished her father would speak again, and rob those last words of their unpleasant significance, but he followed her in silence, striking off, with his aimlessly industrious cane, the brittle, charred twigs that came in his way. When they were nearly opposite the tunnel, the trail widened, and she walked at his side.

" Papa," she said, turning to him brightly, as if to make open amends for her tacit dissatisfaction with him, " why won't you take that Bird off the name of your mine. — Eagle *Bird!*" she repeated, mockingly.

" We'll wait and see who the mine belongs to. Mr. Harkins's taste in names may not be the same as yours."

" Well," said Josephine, " the name is definite enough, if the ownership is vague."

CHAPTER II.

A COMMUNITY OF SPECIALISTS.

An acre of the hill-side above the tunnel had been cleared of its scorched timber to make room for the surface "plant" of the Eagle Bird. The ground was hard and verdureless. Each day's dust, before the next day came, was swept into windrows or whirled away altogether by intermittent gusts, charging up the slope from the valley. The "plant" consisted of the main shaft-house and a number of log-cabins, sheds, and board-houses, grouped irregularly round it. The dwelling of the superintendent was distinguished by its high porch, with an ornamental cornice supporting the eaves, and by the addition of shutters to its windows. Some feeble vines had been early baulked in an attempt to climb the loose warp of strings extending from the railing of the porch to a series of nails ruthlessly driven into the cornice above. Two or three saddle-horses, hitched to the posts which supported the gallery, were swinging their heads discontentedly, and a row of men stood with their backs against the side of the house near the lower entrance, each man with his chin elevated and his hat tilted forward over his eyes, as a defence from the rays of the low sun. Sammis, the temporary superintendent of the Eagle Bird, was holding forth on the subject of the lawsuit to a few friends who had ridden over from the new camp at Spearfish.

As they passed this group Josephine confided to her father in a little grimace her opinion of the gentlemen from Spearfish. She ran up the steps of the piazza, while her father remained below, joining in the talk of the men.

"Say, Mr. Newbold," Sammis appealed to his principal, "I been telling the boys that you bought this here Eagle Bird mine of Jim Keesner, and nobody but him. Is that so, or ain't it?"

"That is so, Sammis," said Mr. Newbold. "The mine was located in Keesner's name, and the transfer of titles was made between him and myself exclusively. Harkins's name was never mentioned. I'm not a mining man, gentlemen," Mr. Newbold continued, smiling upon the company at large, "but I've heard of Colonel Billy Harkins. He's pretty well known in Kansas City."

"He's sold some mines there, I guess," one of the delegation from Spearfish remarked.

"More than he will ever sell there again," said Mr. Newbold. "I never would have touched the property without an expert's report on it, if the colonel's name had been in any way connected with it. I didn't know even that he owned the Uinta."

"The boys here," said Sammis, "was remarkin' it seemed kind o' keerless in you to buy a mine on paper, as you might say. I told 'em you had a copy of the first location notice certified to by the recorder of this district."

"That ought to fix the *title* all right," one of Spearfish men admitted; while another offered the amendment, "If mining records was ever kep' as they'd ought to be, and not sloshed round so public like."

"That's just where I drop on it," said Sammis. "That recorder must 'a' certified to a false copy, or else the record's been tampered with. There isn't a man in camp that don't believe Mr. Newbold owns this mine. Question is, how you goin' to prove it? Why — Lord, when I first got notice to quit work in the new shaft, I didn't pay no more *'tention* to it! I just walked into the court-house one day, and asked to have a look at the location notice of the Eagle Bird mine. And, by —— , there they'd got it all fixed."

"I'd hunt that recorder with a shot-gun!" one of Sammis's friends remarked.

"I wouldn't waste time on him — I'd hunt Jim Keesner," another one said.

"Yes, there'd be more huntin' than findin', I guess," said Sammis. "There's plenty of room between the Rockies and the Sierries for Jim Keesner to hide out. He might be guidin' parties in the mountains; he might be ranchin' it or teamin' it; he might be prospectin' round among the hills somewheres, or down on the reservation; he might 'a' joined them fool Mormons.

"What's Hark' say 's gone of him?" one of the group inquired.

"Harkins? Harkins is as innocent as the babe unborn. He don't know nothin' 'bout Keesner. He just p'ints to his records."

"When I first arrived in the camp," Mr. New-bold interposed, "I should say as many as twenty men came to me and offered to take their affidavit that the Eagle Bird monuments had been moved, and that the change had been made since our big strike here. But come to cross-examine a little, they got all mixed up in their memories. Some remembered one thing, and some one else contradicted it. You couldn't get a single witness who would be worth anything to us out of the whole lot of them.

"Course not," said Sammis. "*I* know them monuments has been moved, but I couldn't prove it to a jury. You don't want memories; you want facts. The facts in this case is — *you* know, Jim," Sammis appealed with a gesture of his thumb to the man who stood next him, "when they first org'nized the district, Shirley Ensign, he called himself, was recorder. P'lonius was the name he went by. Kep' his records in an old candle-box in a corner of The Gem. Then, *you* know, just after they made their big strike up here, The Gem took fire. Of course it was accidental! Harkins packed the records across the street into The Oasis; but it took him a day and a half to get there —"

"What business had he with the records?" Mr. Newbold interrupted.

"Much as anybody," Sammis briefly explained, absorbed in his statement of the situation.

"Where was the recorder?"

"Most likely he was drunk — but, as I was sayin', during the time Colonel Billy had them records he prob'ly looked them over to his advantage. Now, you see," — Sammis sat down on the heels of his boots and drew in the dust with a bit of charred stick two parallelograms side by side, with their boundary-line in common, — "them two claims lay this way. Harkins's workin's was here, and the Eagle Bird had just made a strike right there" — he made two small circles with the bit of stick in the opposite corners of each parallelogram. "The colonel knew them two holes were on the same vein. He just takes them records and floats the north end of his claim right bod'ly to the west'ard, and brings his side line down catercornerin' — that way; and some day when there ain't anybody round, he changes his stakes, and there he's got a first-class legal location right plumb onto your ground." Sammis turned the force of his peroration upon Mr. Newbold. "Oh, the colonel's always legal! He's got his affidavit men always handy. And there's another little peculiarity of his'n you want to keep in mind — he's uncommon lucky in his juries. Now, the man that surveyed them two claims for the location was John Bod'n, and problikely he's got the notes — and also problikely the colonel's got him coppered."

"Sammis, you are a little too figurative for me sometimes," Mr. Newbold mildly observed. "What do you mean by coppered?"

"Bet'n he won't turn up," several voices replied, and every man of the group turned a pitying eye on Mr. Newbold.

Sammis drew the sole of his boot across his diagram, spat upon the smoothed dust, and so rested the case according to the Eagle Bird. The gentlemen from Spearfish, remarking that they had "better be a-movin' on so as to git into camp before dark," mounted their horses and took the lower trail toward the valley.

Mr. Newbold was familiar with the Sammisian theory of the case between the mines, but each fresh exposition of it made him more restive, especially on the point of Bodewin's obduracy.

"Sammis, did you mean to convey by that figure of speech you used just now — "

"That which, sir?"

"That expression you made use of in reference to Bodewin — that Harkins has bought him?"

"Well, sir, I should take Bode'n to be rayther of an expensive article to buy for a man of moderate means; but you can just bet your bottom dollar the colonel's got some holt on him, or he never'd 'a' started the scheme."

" I can force him with a subpœna, if there is no other way to fetch him."

" Well, now, Mr. Newbold, I don't want to give advice, but you don't want to send a sheriff huntin' Bode'n if you mean to git him! He knows this country. He can find his hole and git into it *too* quick." As Sammis became excited, his tone grew more nasal and his speech more untrammelled. " You can't drive him and you can't buy him, in my opinion, — but if you can find Harkins's holt on him — well, I do' know! If you *did* ketch him and force him onto the stand, an unwillin' witness is worse than none."

Mr. Newbold and his daughter rode back to the camp in the splendor of a sunset that loomed red behind the skeleton pines. Josephine let her horse take his own way down the wagon-track, while she watched its dying changes. But she lost the last tints in her preoccupation with the dust and the strange meetings and passings on the broad and level road by which they approached the town. That quickening of the pulse which makes itself felt in every human community as day draws to a close had intensified the life of the camp. The sound of its voices and footsteps, the smoke of its fires, rose in the still, cool air. Cradled between two ranges of the mother mountains of the continent, the little colony could hardly have been more inland in its situation; it had nevertheless in many respects the character of a primitive seaport. It owed its existence to hazardous ventures from a distance. Its shops were filled, not with the fruits of its soil or the labor of its hands, but with cargoes that had been rocked in the four-wheeled merchantmen of the plains. Bronzed-faced, hairy-throated men occupied more than their share of its sidewalks, spending carelessly in a few days and nights the price of months of hardship and isolation. Its hopes and its capital were largely bound up in the fate of adventurers into that unpeopled land which has no history except the records written in fire, in ice, and in water, on its rocks and river-beds; the voyagers across that inland sea where the smoke of lonely camp-fires goes up from wagon-roads that were once hunter's trails, and trails that were once the tracks of buffalo. There were men seen at intervals of many months in its streets, whom the desert and the mountains called, as the sea calls the men of the coast towns. It was a port of the wilderness.

The arrivals due that Saturday night were seeking their dusty moorings. Heavily loaded freighters were lurching in, every mule straining in his collar, every trace taut and quivering. Express-wagons of lighter tonnage took the dust of the freighters, until the width of the road gave their square-trotting draught-horses a chance to swing out and pass. In and out among the craft of heavier burden, shuffled the small, tough bronchos. Their riders were for the most part light built, like their horses, with a bearing at once alert and impassive. They were young men, notwithstanding a prevailing look of care and stolid endurance, due in some cases, possibly, to the dust-laden hollows under the sun-wearied eyes, and to that haggardness of aspect which goes with a beard of a week's growth, a flannel shirt loosely buttoned about a sunburned throat, and a temporary estrangement from soap and water. These were the doughty privateersmen, returning with a convoy of pack-animals from the valley of the Gunnison or the Clearwater, or the tragic hunting-grounds of the Indian Reservation.

Taking the footpath way, beside his loaded donkey trudged the humble "grub-stake," or the haggard-eyed charcoal-burner from his smoking camp in the nearest timber, while far up on the mountain, distinct in the reflected glow of sunset, a puff of white dust appeared from moment to moment, following the curves of the road, where the passenger coach was making its best speed, with brakes hard down, on the home-grade from the summit of the pass.

Mr. Newbold and his daughter entered the town by a side street, and wheeled their horses, at a sharp trot, into the main avenue, a few blocks above the Wiltsie House. The avenue was straight and wide, as befits the avenue of the hopeful future; but the houses were the houses of the uncertain present. They were seldom more than two stories in height, miscellaneous in character, homogeneous in ugliness, crude in newness of paint or rawness of boards without paint. There were frequent breaks in the perspective of their roofs, where a vacant lot awaited its tenant, or the tenant awaited his house. There were tents doing duty for houses; there were skeleton structures hastily clothing themselves with bricks and mortar that meantime impeded the sidewalk. One-half of the street was torn up for the laying of gas-pipes, and crossings were occasionally blockaded by the bulk of a house on rollers, which night had overtaken in its snail-like progress. The passing crowd was a crowd distinguished by a predominance of boots and hats — dusty or muddy boots, and hats with a look of preternatural age or of startling newness. There was a dearth of skirts; and these, when they appeared, were given a respectful, an almost humorously respectful, share of the sidewalk. The crowd went its way with none of that smart unanimity of movement which characterizes the up-town and down-town march of feet trained to the pavement. It slouched and straggled and stared, and stopped in the middle of the common way, and greeted its friends, and vociferated its sentiments, and exhibited its ore-specimens of fabulous promise, regardless of incommoded passers. It was invariably good-natured.

Two distinct groups were forming in the street: one, small and shifting, in front of the Wiltsie House, expecting the hourly arrival of the stage; and one larger, more persevering and disorderly, on the corner opposite the Variety Theatre, where a band of music was playing airs of a rather belated popularity. Spanning the street, between the upper windows of the theatre and the opposite roof, a tight rope was stretched against the fading flush of sunset, and a Mademoiselle Cordova (whose colors were also fading, but were capable of resuscitation for the evening's performance) was advertised to make her *début* in the camp upon this rope. Here the expectant evening stir reached a climax of excitement, and beyond it suddenly ceased. In fact, the town ceased. There was nothing more but the stage on which its shabby little drama was set. Its lights were lowered; the wind of evening, of coolness and vast space, drew through its lofty wings. Ranging down the valley, peak beyond peak, the mountains lifted their illumined heads.

"The sunset is gone!" Josephine exclaimed; "but what a night — oh, what a night! Papa, do look at the mountains!" she shouted, trying to catch his ear in the noise of the street.

"Never mind the mountains, — look out for that freighter!" her father replied. "You can't ride here as if you were on Wabash Avenue."

A little later she tried again, "Papa, where do you suppose they all come from?"

They had halted at the edge of the sidewalk,

and Josephine was gazing around her at the moving mass of male humanity, while her father dismounted with circumspection.

"Oh, they are the superfluous people from everywhere."

"Why, of course! Just like us. I never felt more superfluous in my life!"

Laughing as she leaned from her saddle, with her hands on her father's shoulders, she dropped lightly to the ground, and the door inscribed "Ladies' Entrance Wiltsie House" closed behind her.

The Newbolds usually dined late, on a theory that by so doing they escaped the greatest crowd, in the only dining-room of the hotel. Josephine had changed her dress and was moving about in the solitude of the ladies' parlor, looking at the desolate chromos on its walls, and sitting in unquiet attitudes on its blue-velvet chairs, when her father entered. He was looking fatigued, and with the tired expression the lines of his face lapsed into a heaviness which emphasized the contrast between father and daughter as they stood opposite each other. Mr. Newbold's proportions were conspicuously inelegant, while Josephine stood lightly on her feet, her small dark head nearly as high as her father's. Her low-browed, round-cheeked face, with its long sweep of eyebrow, short, full mouth, and rich coloring, would have been excessively pretty, wanting its candid brightness of expression and the dark eyes which gave it dignity. With these, it was quite enough to have convinced Bodewin of the fatuity of local prejudices where girls are concerned.

Mr. Newbold had entered the room preoccupied with an idea which had struck him as a good one from several points of view.

" Josephine," he began, in pursuance of this idea, " wouldn't it rather amuse you to *meet* Bodewin ? "

Josephine stared at him.

" He is one of the types of the place, you know," he continued, resolutely. " Not the red-flannel shirt and revolver style, but something a little more subtle, as you would say. A kind of a Yankee lotus-eater."

Josephine was struck by a somewhat awkward deliberation in her father's manners. The word Yankee coming from him also displeased her in a way she felt to be childish. Her mother and her mother's people had been Yankees, so called. As she remained silent, her father added at random : —

"You are a student of human nature, you know."

"I, papa?" Josephine laughed uncomfortably. "What put that into your head? All the human nature I ever tried to study was my own, which is certainly human. I am not looking for types; I shouldn't know one if I saw it. If you mean, would I like you to introduce Mr. Bodewin to me, no, papa, thank you, decidedly I would not. I hate to make acquaintances in that premeditated way."

"Well, well! It's hardly likely you would *know* Bodewin — I only thought he might help you to pass the time while we are here, and the chance of talking with a nice, bright girl in a place like this would be a boon to any fellow."

"He has not shown himself very eager for the chance," said Josephine. "Besides, papa, if he is going to be so disagreeable about your lawsuit, I don't know why we should be civil to him."

Mr. Newbold reflected that a little timely civility might go far to overcome Bodewin's disagreeableness, but he wisely kept this reflection to himself. Josephine was unsophisticated, as all men, however wise in their generation, like their women to be.

CHAPTER III.

MRS. CRAIG'S LITTLE DINNER.

"When will you come up?" Mr. Craig asked of Mr. Newbold the next afternoon, as his client was leaving the office of Joseph Craig, counsel for the Eagle Bird against Lee and Harkins. "We want you to come before the Government Survey moves into its new quarters. The party are in camp now in the woods back of our cabin. There is no better company this side of the range than you'll get round their camp-fire of an evening. No ceremony — pot of beans or oatmeal or what not, boiling on the coals for to-morrow's breakfast — boys in their buckskins — not one of them but your daughter might dance with, or dine with, or gallop across country with, as she happened to find them. They're liable to turn up almost anywhere, those fellows — at the swell clubs in New York or London, or the President's receptions, or digging their way up some mountain-peak above snow-line."

"I hope I shall never meet any of them there!"
Mr. Newbold interjected.

"No," laughed Mr. Craig, "it isn't likely you
will. I never met any of them there myself.
Well, when will you come? Thursday? Thursday then. We are only camping within four
walls ourselves. We can't ask you to *dine*."

"We can hardly be said to dine at the Wiltsie
House."

"No, it's a good time to take you, after a fortnight at the Wiltsie. You must have forgotten
how the flesh-pots tasted. Tell Miss Newbold to
put on a pair of stout boots, and after dinner we
will go over to the Camp of the Geologists and
get Hillbury talking, if we can."

"My daughter will be delighted. She gets
restless these moonlight nights, because she
cannot be out-of-doors. It is too bad to be shut
up in a third-rate hotel with such a country as
this around us. *I* don't know where to take her.
I'm half tempted sometimes to give the young
fellows round here a chance to amuse her. I'm
not much of a rider, or much of a climber, myself.
She wants to get up on top some of those peaks,
and she wants to go down in a mine."

"Of course she does; and you can't find any

better fellows to trust her with than Hillbury's crowd. If she wants a chaperon, my wife will go along with her any time you like to get up a party."

"It's very kind of you, Craig, I'm sure." Mr. Newbold had buttoned his coat and taken up his hat and cane. He stood, tapping the one against the other, while Mr. Craig spoke to a clerk who had stepped to the door of his private office. "How about Bodewin?" he said, as the door closed and Mr. Craig turned back to his desk.

"Bodewin? There's nothing new about Bodewin that I know of."

"Have we got to give him up?"

"Not at all. We can't give him up. There's the subpœna, when we're ready for it."

"I don't like that. I don't think we'll gain anything by it. Now, Sammis has an idea in his head once in a while. He says it's no use to try the subpœna on Bodewin. He'd manage to leak out; or, as he puts it, an unwilling witness is worse than none."

"This is not a question of verbal testimony," Mr. Craig rejoined. "Bodewin can be required to produce certain papers which he is pretty well understood to have had in his possession when

Harkins first made his claim, and it was known you would resist it. Now, if he has the papers, that is all we want. If he has destroyed them since the dispute about the records came up, he must have had some reason for doing so. He can be required to give it. Don't you see? IIis unwillingness is a strong point in our favor — the more obvious the unwillingness, the stronger the point. He does not intend to appear against Harkins — that I'm tolerably sure of. Money won't fetch him. There is some personal hitch."

"I'd like to know what it is."

"So would I. But I don't think we ever will know — from Bodewin."

"Has Bodewin any 'pard,' as you say out here, or any intimate friend in the camp?"

"I don't think he has any intimate friends here, except Hillbury of the Survey. He was on the Survey himself, under Wheeler. As for a 'pard,' Bodewin is a gentlemen, as you say back there."

"What I am getting at," said Mr. Newbold, "is whether Bodewin is among his friends here, where he would be likely to talk about his affairs now and then when he felt communicative, or whether he is shut up in himself. According to my small experience of men, I believe that almost every man, even the most reticent, once in a while, perhaps, will talk to some one. The shyer he is and the longer he has been locked up, the more likely he is to open out to the right one, if the right one happens to come along at the right time. Now, with Bodewin, if we could get at his scruple, whatever it is, it would be a great point gained. I don't like this subpœna. I don't like it at all — with a man like him. You don't know what turn he might take. It's too much like a Jack-in-the-box — you open the box, and the thing is out in spite of you. The right way is to get at his reasons, whatever they are, and meet them — talk him out of them. But you can't argue with a man when you don't know your premises."

"Mr. Newbold, I don't know what influence you may have with Bodewin, but I can't flatter myself, from what I know of him, that I'm the right one to induce him to unburden himself."

"Nor I either, my dear sir. Now, between us both, I shouldn't wonder if it were a case for a woman."

"D——a woman!" Mr. Craig now turned from his desk and gave his fullest attention to his client's rambling remarks. "What woman do you propose to introduce into the case?"

"Well," said Mr. Newbold, disconcertedly, "I haven't any in view at this moment. But I suppose Bodewin is not the kind of man to be influenced by a woman who wasn't a — well — a lady."

"Oh! If it is a case for a lady's influence, you will hardly need any legal adviser."

Mr. Craig turned back to his desk and began to pull about his papers.

"My dear Craig, — hold on! You're taking me too seriously altogether, I assure you. It is of no consequence — only a suggestion. I hate to leave the camp with the thing in the shape it's in now."

"Leave the thing to me, Mr. Newbold, — and leave the woman out of it if you please. I think myself, you'd much better stay and see it through. You'll be better satisfied, you know."

"I dare say you are right."

"I wish you *would* stay until after the trial. You'll see some fun. Mining law is peculiar," Mr. Craig called after his client. He had not taken the trouble to see him to the door.

Mr. Newbold had been advised, in his choice of counsel, to employ a man of local knowledge and reputation rather than one more widely known in the profession. Each State, each mining district even, had its own mining laws, and few busy lawyers, however well read, could keep informed of all these various "local regulations and customs."

Mr. Craig was a small man, too nervous and irritable for a lawyer, with a large head, a complexion of reddish fairness, and a peremptory, careless manner, cultivated in provincial Western circles. He had been educated at an Indiana college, and going East soon afterwards, on the usual pilgrimage which the complacent young West makes, at least once in its life, to the old, sad, unprosperous homes of its conservative Eastern relatives, — critical even in their decline, — had fallen in love with a second or third cousin, a surprisingly lively young person for the only girl left in a large, elderly, and peculiar family connection.

It still remained a wholesome mystery to him how he had managed to persuade this young woman to go West with him. She had seemed to him the cleverest girl he had ever met, and the most insensible to masculine attractions. She had laughed at his little egotisms and provincialisms, and at a later stage of their acquaintance had fiercely maintained the superiority of the most commonplace Eastern existence over the most triumphant career life could offer west of the Little Miami. And yet she had married him. Her friends considered that she had thrown herself away, both as to the man and his circumstances; for even in the most figurative sense Joseph Craig could hardly be regarded as a type of that vast material prosperity of the West his Eastern relatives found, in theory, so revolting. Mrs. Craig had expected that she would make a great change in her husband, if not in her husband's circumstances. She would make him wear darker clothes and smaller hats, and reform him of a habit of leaning on the hind legs of his chair, and of passing his hand over his hair in the pauses of conversation. She would make him see the logic of free trade, and persuade him to read Emerson and Herbert Spencer instead of so many newspapers. She would insist upon less prominence in his final r's. They had now been married nine years, but no change as yet was evident in Craig, except that he was growing stout and slightly bald. Mrs. Craig's complexion had lost its delicate New England bloom in the strong Western suns and winds; she had grown thin instead of stout, and her soft frail light locks were scarcely abundant enough to make the small low knot which was fashion's modest demand at that time. But she met all changes for the worse in her appearance with rather a defiant honesty, secure in the conviction that "Joe" liked her just as she was. She was as lively and inconsistent as ever, as vociferously opposed to her husband in theory, and as vehemently his partisan in practice. She was restless, merry, moody, wearing herself out over her work or her play; overestimating or underestimating her friends and her own circumstances; enthusiastic over her children's promise or in despair over their performance. Mr. Craig had that immense respect for his profession that an unknown Western lawyer with a decidedly unlegal turn of mind might be expected to have. This was one of his idiosyncrasies which his wife had never laughed at him about. Clever and keen as she was, she had never yet seen her husband quite as others saw him, and happily took as serious a view of him professionally as he did of himself.

Mr. Craig was absolutely, almost vindictively, honest. He had many, in fact most, of the paramount virtues, but he was one of those men who are elected to be poor, to be unpopular, and to be held at less than their actual worth.

The Craig household, like many another on the frontier, was conducted on the theory of "catastrophism" rather than that of "uniform law." The dinner to the Newbolds happened to occur on one of its days of "convulsive upheaval." Mrs. Craig's butcher had betrayed her, her greengrocer had "gone back on her," her cook had stabbed her to the heart's core of her housewifery pride. Finally, her eldest boy, a three-year-old, had tumbled into the hydraulic ditch which flowed past the house, — at a temperature of melted snow, — had been dragged, dripping and gasping, into the house, about twenty minutes before the dinner-hour, stripped of his clothes, hastily scolded, and rubbed down with brandy and rough towels in front of a scorching fire in the dining, reception, and only living room of the house, and tucked into his bed as the guests arrived at the door. The maid-of-all-work opened the door, while Mrs. Craig swept up the towels in one arm, and retreated to her bedroom, holding the boy's wet garments at arm's length. With scarlet cheeks, a rather dubious smile of welcome, and with an irrepressible odor of brandy per-

vading her garments, she appeared before her
guests a moment later, shutting out a burst of infant wrath and dolor, as she closed the door behind her. The soft-hearted Irish servant, who
was putting the last touches to the table, was so
distracted by these sounds that she could hardly
be induced to remember she had other duties
besides those of consolation. The nurse had
been sent to the camp to inquire into the non-
appearance of the fruit which had been ordered
for dessert.

It was an inauspicious beginning to an extremely bad little dinner. Fitful bursts of gayety
from the hostess alternated with sudden silences,
during which her eyes wandered anxiously towards
her husband's face. Coffee was served at last,
and the company turned its chairs from the table
to the fire. Mr. Craig went in search of a box of
cigars, and the evening cleared up with a promise
of cheerfulness if not of brilliancy.

There was still the visit to Mr. Hillbury's camp
to redeem the failure of the dinner. Mrs. Craig
perhaps overvalued the picturesque in the absence
of the comfortable, but she had been moderately
comfortable all her life, and had only since her
marriage begun to be even remotely picturesque.

CHAPTER IV.

THE CAMP-FIRE.

THE Craig cabin stood on a narrow peninsula of roughly cleared ground, with the pine woods behind it. It was characteristic of mining nomenclature that the stream of pure swift-running water, which formed this peninsula, taken from the infant Arkansas, should be called a "ditch." The path which ran beside it was called, in the same concise nomenclature, the "ditch walk." It was a favorite promenade of the camp. It commanded a view of the sunset behind the pine woods, of the camp in the gulch, and of the mountains which rose beyond, taking upon their worn, sphinx-like faces the sun's descending glow. Mrs. Craig had walked off more than one imperative fit of weeping there — nervous weeping, without assignable cause, unless it might be a dumb awe and terror of her surroundings, as if several layers of the earth's crust had been torn away, and she, with a modern woman's oversensi-

tiveness and complicated needs, had been dropped
upon one of the primeval strata, with huge dumb
forms of unknown life around her. The mountains themselves had, to her morbid fancy, an op-
pressive individuality. They intruded upon her,
in the midst of her small, subtle joys and pains of
to-day, with their heart-breaking stolidity and
their immense past. They took the meaning out
of her efforts, and made them seem of no avail.
When she tried to express these fancies to her
husband, he received them into his masculine consciousness as a phase of her own idiosyncrasy,
in spite of her assurance that every other woman
in the camp probably had the same. That evening, as she kept the path by Josephine in the
moonlight, she had no fancies that were not
cheerful. Perhaps it came of the contact with a
younger, stronger, and simpler woman's nature.
Perhaps she was healthfully tired from her
domestic difficulties, and enjoying that slumber of
nerves which comes with honest bodily fatigue.
The mountains looked to her only solemn and
beautiful, and were simply a noble range of peaks
guarding a valley filled with moonlit haze.
The moon, peering behind the pine trunks, had
no expression beyond that of the full moon, half

an hour risen. Under her sense of the beauty around her was the happy thought of a wife who sees a remarkable proof of her husband's goodness in his least and most natural act. There was not another man in the world, she felt sure, who would not have been furious over such a grotesque failure as her dinner had been. She hurried Josephine gayly along, and now they stopped on the edge of the wood to wait for the men, who had followed more slowly. A sound of wind came from the gulch, distant at first, creeping from tree to tree, making a sudden hurry and shivering rush in the trees above their heads, and stealing away again down the dim slope towards the valley.

"Yes, that is the camp," she said, in reply to a question from Josephine. "Take care of those pine-stubs — you cannot see them with the light in your eyes; won't you take hold of my hand?"

"Won't you take hold of mine?" laughed Josephine. "I am ever so much taller than you."

"Yes, but I know the ground. I walk here hours and hours by myself. There is no one in camp all day except the cook, who is generally asleep in one of the wagons; but the tents, and the mules stamping and munching, make it seem less lonely in the woods. That is Mr. Hillbury — the dark head against the tent-curtain; he is the chief of this party, you know. You must notice his buckskins. They are Indian-tanned, made by a London tailor. We have to amuse ourselves with these little contrasts — they are the spice of life out here."

Mr. Hillbury, hearing the footsteps and voices approaching, came out to meet his guests, saying, "Who are these in bright array?" He looked extremely well in his suit of buckskin, which was of a light-gray color, toned by use, and set off his dark complexion as if chosen for that purpose alone. There was the usual indistinct mention of names as the group of young men around the fire rose to their feet. The camp lamented its deficiencies in the matter of seats. There was but one camp-stool, which, both ladies declining, was bestowed by acclamation on Mr. Newbold. "I'm the oldest and heaviest," he declared, and accepted it on that basis. The other seats were sections of pine logs with boards nailed across the top. Mrs. Craig, seeing Josephine balancing herself on one of these inverted pedestals, called to her to come and share with her a camp-blanket spread on the ground. A man reclining on one elbow near them, with his feet to the fire and his face in deep shadow, gathered himself into a sitting posture and gave them good-evening.

"Good-evening, Mr. Bodewin; were you here when we came?" asked Mrs. Craig, leaning forward and speaking across Josephine's lap.

"Yes, Mrs. Craig. I got up and made my bow with the rest, but the fire was between us."

"I did not see you," said Mrs. Craig — "Miss Newbold, this is Mr. Bodewin."

Bodewin moved nearer, first knocking the hot ashes out of a brier-wood pipe and thrusting it, bowl downward, into a breast-pocket of his coat. "Poor Mr. Bodewin!" said Mrs. Craig, noting the action sympathetically. "As the wife of a smoker I can feel for you. You had found such a nice place to finish your pipe in silence and in peace; now we have interrupted your pipe and broken your silence."

"There is always something to be thankful for, Mrs. Craig," Bodewin replied. "You might have interrupted the silence and broken the pipe."

Josephine was listening less to Bodewin's words than to his voice, low-pitched and rather languid, with an accent that was negligently pure. His face she could not see without turning, too evidently, to look at him.

Perceiving that she had a neighbor on her right, Mrs. Craig began talking to him, and the group thus divided itself.

"How you must enjoy this life!" said Josephine, filling the pause with the first words she could think of.

Before answering, Bodewin deliberately shifted his position so that it commanded a view of her face, one-half of its beauty revealed in the firelight, the other suggested in shadow.

"Do you mean the life of the Survey?" he asked.

"Yes," she said.

"It is a good life, no doubt, but it is not mine."

"I thought you were of this party."

Bodewin fancied that he had lost a degree of her interest by this admission. He could see her bright eyes exploring the circle of dimly seen faces around the camp-fire, and doubted not she was already idealizing their owners in true girl-fashion, and imparting to the life they led all the picturesqueness she found in its accidental surroundings.

"No," he repeated, with his lazy intonation, "I am not a mining geologist, nor a physical geologist, nor a geological physicist, nor even a supernumerary on board wages."

" That is what I should like to be — that last."

" Why, if you please ? "

" It must be so easy to earn board wages — especially — "

" When the board is rather bad ? "

" They are *not* wildly luxurious, are they ? " she whispered.

" No ; the pursuit of science under government is not a luxurious calling. However, it is but fair to the government to say that this is but a temporary arrangement. The Survey goes under cover next week, and I dare say they will have a few chairs."

" Mr. Bodewin, haven't *you* some capital letters after your name ? "

" After my name, Miss Newbold? When had my name the honor to be seen by you ? "

" I think it was — about two weeks ago — in a letter to you from my father," she hesitated, conscious of a somewhat awkward reason for the question she had asked — " and the letters were M. E."

"I believe I am entitled to C. E. after my name, but the M. E. must have been a friendly flight of imagination on your father's part."

"Are you not a mining expert?"

"I have been so called. But I believe there is no such title in the back of the dictionary."

"Who is talking about dictionaries by the light of a camp-fire?" Mrs. Craig exclaimed, adding her profuse treble to the duet. "Are you beginning at the fountain-head of conversation in the English language.? If Miss Newbold were a Boston girl I should be sure she had a dictionary — a German dictionary — in her trunk, even if it crowded out her best bonnet."

"I'm sure there's no best bonnet in my trunk," said Josephine. "Perhaps I ought to be ashamed to say I brought but two books with me, and those I can read without the aid of a dictionary — even an English one."

Mrs. Craig thought the contents of a traveller's trunk were next to a biography of its owner. "It represents his necessities, the things he cannot leave behind. If we knew those two books Miss Newbold chooses out of all those she leaves at home, we should know Miss Newbold."

"Suppose she makes a good choice but doesn't

read the books after she has brought them?" Josephine said.

" Then we should know her aspirations. They are as much a part of us as our necessities, surely."

" The part a biographer usually leaves out," Bodewin said. " How about the traveller who hasn't necessities enough to fill a trunk? How would you write his biography, Mrs. Craig?"

"Oh, a man who has no trunk cannot expect to have a biography. Practically, he doesn't exist."

Following the silence Mrs. Craig's peremptory little speech had made, Josephine asked:

" Will you tell me, Mr. Bodewin, what a mining expert *is*, granting that M. E. doesn't stand for him, and that he isn't in the back of the dictionary ?"

" He is, usually, a gentleman who asks a good deal of money to tell you how little he knows, or perhaps, I might add, how much less some other man knows."

" That is a rather unsatisfactory description."

" A mining expert is frequently a. rather unsatisfactory person. But there is a difference in experts, as in other people, and perhaps it is but fair to remember that in forming their conclusions they have to deal with Nature in some of her most unaccountable and fantastic moods. The experience gained in examining ninety-nine different formations may be of no use in the one-hundredth. It is a business no man can say he has . learned absolutely."

"Then why do they charge so much for knowledge which is not knowledge? Is it because of the risk to their reputations in saying a thing is true, while they really take the chance of its being otherwise?"

"Hardly that, I should say," said Bodewin, a little bored by the effort to give conscientious answers to questions that did not fit his mood, but willing to humor a pretty girl's thirst for information. "An honest expert charges for the responsibility he takes in giving such opinions as he is able to form from his experience and study. If the responsibility is great he charges accordingly."

Josephine was mentally referring Bodewin's words to her father's case, — a case where facts alone were called for, not experience or responsibility or study; and the five thousand dollars her father had offered, and Bodewin had refused, would suggest, in spite of herself, a very ugly word.

Mr. Hillbury, from the other side of the fire, leaned forward and threw on it another log. The wind veered and carried the smoke of the augmented flame into their faces. They scrambled, laughing, to their feet, and retreated, Bodewin dragging the blanket after him. He spread it down again on the windward side of the fire, but Josephine did not seem disposed to resume her seat.

They were hovering about in that fascinating borderland between firelight and moonlight. The moon had risen high enough to fill the thin woods with its light; but it was a pale, suffused radiance by contrast with the red fire-glow. The wind in the tree-tops over their heads, like a circle of unseen whisperers, closed around the lightly joined thread of their talk.

"Do people ever get used to this?" Josephine asked.

"I am afraid they do. But they enjoy it over again, as I do to-night, seeing your fresh eyes take it all in for the first time."

"How do you know that I like it? I have not said so, have I?"

"I can see that you do."

"I do, I do!" she said, in her full, cordial tones. "But not all of it."

"No; there is too much of it to be all good." After a pause he asked: "Your father is making a longer stay in the camp than he intended, is he not?"

"Yes; we were to have gone this week. He will wait now until after the trial."

"I hope he will gain his suit," Bodewin said civilly.

"Do you?" came involuntarily from Josephine.

"Why are you surprised, Miss Newbold, to find my sympathies on the side of justice?"

"I did not know you thought that was our side," Josephine replied coldly.

"I do think so."

"Then if you care about justice, why don't you go into court and say so?"

Josephine looked at him, hardly less astonished than he at her own words. It was undeniably careless of Bodewin to have assumed that Miss Newbold knew nothing of his connection with her father's lawsuit. And Josephine, under the pressure of her own misgivings, had allowed herself to be goaded by his cool allusion into an extraordinary liberty. So she instantly felt it to be, and so she knew that he also regarded it. He looked at her keenly and gravely.

" You must not answer that question," she said. " I had no right to ask it."

" Perhaps you had not," he assented. " You will pardon me if I do not answer it."

" You will only humiliate me if you do."

Neither found it easy to go on talking as they had talked before. By a common impulse they moved back towards the camp, and when they rejoined the circle around the fire, Josephine contrived that her seat should be as far away as possible from Bodewin. Her evening was spoiled —and more than that. She did not ask herself what more, but miserably she felt what a fire is the tongue that is not disciplined. It had not occurred to her before whether she was likely or not to meet Bodewin again, but now she found herself earnestly hoping that she might. She longed to retrieve herself, for the sake of her own self-respect. Mr. Hillbury was telling a story in his low, pleasant tones and matter-of-fact manner that heightened the effect of his climaxes. She tried to fix her attention upon it, and sat with a strained half-smile on her face and her eyes on the speaker, never looking at or speaking to Bodewin again, except to say good-evening to him in her quietest manner when the company broke up.

Bodewin lingered after the other guests had gone, and smoked another pipe with Hillbury. The latter remarked upon Miss Newbold's beauty. It was too obvious to call for discussion, though Hillbury invited one by saying that she was too unconscious to be thoroughly graceful, and that to him she seemed like a preposterously handsome boy.

"Oh, come!" said Bodewin. "If she were *coquette* with that face and figure, where should we be? Heaven is merciful, after all!"

When the pipe was finished Bodewin took his way along the ditch walk alone. The Craig cabin was dark as he passed it. He stopped on the foot-bridge and leaned upon the rail, watching the current slide under the shadow of the bridge and out again into the light. A reflection of the moon, now high overhead, floated in the black water of the ditch. It wavered and widened and shrunk, as the water shifted its levels under the golden gleam. It struck Bodewin as a rather dreary thing that he should have been so startled by a girl's impulsive question. It showed how seldom girls had taken the trouble to ask him questions, even uncomplimentary ones, about himself. Well, it wasn't so disagreeable for a first experience of the kind. Its novelty was not its only charm. He half wished, now that it was too late, that he had tried to answer her question, and so admitted in some sort her right to ask it. It might have ended in a rather piquant flirtation on high moral grounds, since they were to be so much longer together in the camp; but now there was small likelihood of any concession on her part. She had without doubt the true woman's art to punish a man for her own offence against him.

CHAPTER V.

MISS NEWBOLD'S opportunity to retrieve herself came, not many days later, through the innocent machinations of Mrs. Craig. Mrs. Craig also wished to retrieve herself. She had given the Newbolds a bad dinner. Atonement was out of the question where Mr. Newbold was concerned, unless it might be through making Mr. Newbold's daughter happy. Her head had not touched her pillow, the night after the dinner, before it began comparing rides and walks and excursions in various directions, with a view to Miss Newbold's amusement. Chance, after all, decided her choice. Mr. Hillbury offered a professional errand of his own as an excuse for a ride half-way to the top of one of the famed peaks of the neighboring range. A party was quickly made up. Mr. Newbold at the outset declined to attempt a twenty-mile ride on horseback including a good deal of mountain work; but he was obviously pleased with the

64

plan, for his daughter's sake. Bodewin was invited, Mrs. Craig informing him that he was expected to supply those minor passages without which a pleasure party, like dance music, is flat.

"We are all monotonously major, every one of us, — Mr. Hillbury, Miss Newbold, Joe, and myself. You must come along and change the key."

The riders made an early start from the Wiltsie House. Mr. Newbold stood on the curbstone and watched them out of sight, Josephine taking the lead, with Mr. Craig on her right and Hillbury on her left, followed by Mrs. Craig with Bodewin beside her, on his bald-faced bay. Half a mile beyond the camp they left the stage-road for one of the many stony trails which climbed the sides of the gulch, branching in various directions towards as many different mines. Always ascending northward, they crossed the belt of burnt timber and entered the dark and fragrant spruce woods, the last and toughest growth on the mountain-side. Here they rode singly in a green twilight chinked with golden lights. The trail was barely distinguishable; the horses' hoofs fell with a soft thud on the thick-sifted layers of spruce needles, or struck, with a hollow ring, the trunk of a fallen tree in stepping over it. No bird-calls broke the stillness; no sounds of any kind betrayed the small furtive activities of forest habitants. It was late, even for the season of wild flowers fed from the cold-bosomed snows of the range. A few patches of the inextinguishable fire-weed lighted the dim slopes; and occasionally, beside the trail, there bloomed in its weird beauty a poppy-shaped flower on a long hair-like stem with petals colored like the wings of a lunar moth.

From time to time Josephine, riding ahead, tried the silence shyly with her voice. It was a voice with one or two exquisite notes in it beside the note, ever welcome, of youth. It was like a human response to the dumb litany of the forest. Josephine was happy to be on horseback in a new and singularly interesting, if not always beautiful, region. The keen edge had passed from her mortification with regard to Bodewin. She was content to let him keep his impressions of her, however unfortunate they might be, without any effort on her part to correct them, so long as a morning as perfect as this found her still in tune. So healthy and so honest a girl could not keep her head low because of a single slip, which hurt her through her delicacy rather than her conscience, and merely affected her passing relations with a stranger. In forgiving herself, she forgave Bodewin, and was at peace with the world. Nevertheless, stranger as he was, she wished, before he drifted out of her life altogether, that he could be cleared of the reproach which still clung to him in her thoughts. Was it through listlessness merely and vain obliviousness that he kept silent when the truth was demanded of him? Was it likely that in the past his life-threads had become entangled with those of Harkins — a man whom common report called an unscrupulous rogue, though a merry one, and generous enough with his spoils when won? What could there be in common between them? Yet she constantly heard it said that Bodewin would not appear against Harkins. Why not? Well, let it go! She was sure to do some one, perhaps more than one, some horrible injustice in her thoughts, if she let them dwell on this subject, which had already proved a pitfall to her discretion.

"Isn't she charming?" Mrs. Craig said to Bodewin. The trees parting had allowed him to keep at her side. "So extravagantly pretty, and yet so simple and womanly! Don't you think so?"

"I have not tried epithets on her yet," Bodewin replied. "But I dare say I could find fault with yours. I should not call her extravagantly pretty, and I doubt if it would be safe to rely on her simplicity."

"Oh, I don't mean that kind of simplicity! She is simple like an antique, like a young goddess."

"Which one do you mean?" he said. "There is the Goddess of Liberty on the Capitol. Do you call her simple?"

"No, I call her decidedly ornate. There is a word which just describes her if I could only think of it."

"Do you mean the Goddess of Liberty?"

"No, I mean my goddess."

"Perhaps western is the word you want."

"Western? Well, it isn't such a bad word if you take it right."

"I mean it right."

"Somehow I cannot talk to you this morning, Mr. Bodewin, I think you are not in your happiest vein. Are you?"

"I have no happy veins, Mrs. Craig. They all 'pinched out' years ago."

"Sink a new shaft then, and prospect for more. Isn't that good advice?"

"If one had any new ground to sink on. The really virtuous thing to do would be to overhaul the old dumps and try to make days' wages out of them."

"You'll never be so virtuous as that! The American does not live who is content with days' wages merely at anything."

"It is time he was born then," said Bodewin.

"Don't be so dismal! It is uncomplimentary, and it isn't patriotic. When you see a girl like that from Kansas City, doesn't it make you feel how rich the country must be in girls?"

Bodewin laughed. "If it be not rich for me —" and then the trees crowding them apart, he lifted his hat and dropped behind. When next they met, Mrs. Craig took up the burden briskly, the theme being still the same.

"She's not a Kansas City girl, you know."

"No?"

"No, she is not a Missourian. It would be strange if she were, even in name. Her family — that is her mother's family — have no cause to love them. Her mother's father was shot dead — on his own doorstep, if you please — by a mob of Missourians during the border troubles."

"An unpleasant little incident in the family history, I should say."

"Unpleasant! Ah, it must take a good many generations for a shock like that to die out of the blood! And there was trouble enough before it came to the shooting, — journeys and hardships and struggles and excitements. You don't ask what his offence was!"

"I suppose his offence was that he was a Free-State settler."

"A brave and consistent one; yes. He was one of that band of families who were turned back by the cannon planted on the Missouri River to prevent the steamboats from landing Free-State men. They went north by way of Iowa and Nebraska (a cheerful little journey), and when they reached the border again, they were met by government soldiers and deprived of their arms as if they had been a band of convicts. No one, it seems, ever thought of disarming the Missourians. The grandfather Fletcher, Joseph Fletcher, — hence Josephine, — had signed a protest against the shameless election frauds. They came to his house one night and demanded to search the premises for incendiary books and papers. The New York 'Tribune' would have been incendiary, I suppose, in those days, or Whittier's poems. He refused to let them in. He told them his wife was very ill —"

"Was she?"

"Of course she was, — so ill that she died soon afterwards. They accused him of signing the protest. He did not deny it, and they then politely informed him that they would not disturb his wife that night, but would trouble him to go with them. They were going to tar and feather him, or do something hideous to him."

"How did he know that?"

"I suppose they told him. At all events he refused to go with them. Wouldn't you have refused?"

"Possibly I should."

"You know you would — any man would! They tried to compel him; he resisted, and they shot him. The family were desired not to pollute the territory with their presence any longer. Their friends the Missourians escorted them to the border, — the wife, two grown sons, and Miss Josephine's mother, then a girl of sixteen. At some little town in Ohio they buried their mother. The sons remained there, and are now wealthy men in Cleveland. The daughter married Mr.

Newbold. I cannot imagine how he ever persuaded her to go back with him to Kansas, but he did, after the sacking and shooting were over. Josephine was born at Wyandot. She is just as old as the Free-State Constitution."

"Did Miss Newbold tell you this story, Mrs. Craig?"

"No; oh, no! That would not be like her, I am sure. Mr. Newbold told it to Mr. Craig one day when they were alone together in the office. He was speaking of his wife's delicate health, and the trial it was for Josephine to leave her. But Mrs. Newbold, it seems, has a perfect horror of the frontier; I should think she would have. When she found her husband bent on this trip, she insisted Josephine should bear him company; to take care of him, I suppose, if he should be ill. He spoke very nicely about his wife, Mr. Craig said; but I dare say he couldn't help being a little complacent over her anxiety about himself. Miss Newbold has never mentioned her mother to me but once. She told me that her mother was born among the mountains, that she had never seen them since her childhood, and often dreamed of them with a homesick longing; that she wanted her, Josephine, to see them and be among them while she was still a girl. I think that is so natural; and of course she would not say it to her husband."

"Wouldn't she? Why not?"

"Could she talk about her dreams of the old home in the East she never expected to see again, to a man like Mr. Newbold?"

"Perhaps she does not take the same view of Mr. Newbold that you do. At all events, she was willing at one time to exchange those dreams for a reality which must have been something like him."

"Ah! that was the husband of her youth. Does he look like the husband of anybody's youth? He has deteriorated. He has let himself down, you may be sure of that. He has that sleek, prosperous blood in him."

"You think there are no martyrs on Mr. Newbold's side?"

"I should say, judging from papa Newbold, that as a family they would be distinguished by good digestions and a tendency to conform whenever opposition was likely to make things uncomfortable. However, I can't be just to him. I gave him such a horrible little dinner, and we never can forgive the people we have irretrievably wronged."

CHAPTER VI.

THEY had now left the heavy timber behind them. The firs grew more sparsely and were low and crooked; occasionally the weather-worn trunk of a dead tree leaned in spectral whiteness against the dark ranks of its survivors. The riders were close upon the line where trees cease and vegetation creeps close to the ground and takes a fur-like habit. Against the deep, cloudless blue of the upper atmosphere rose the brown and naked peaks, streaked with supernal snows. The sun glowed hot upon them; motionless shadows defined every angle and chasm. Clear, solid masses of shadow swept down the sheer slopes into the cañon. They were now twelve thousand feet above the level of the sea, crossing a shoulder of the mountain, from which they looked down into deep below deep of shadow and light, descending to the map-like picture of river-laced valley and high, barren plain, mesa, and mountain, range beyond range, brown and purple and blue, departing towards the infinite distance. The horses panted, their ears drooped, their hoofs rattled on the rocky planes up which they clambered. There was no soil and no verdure except a dry, iron-stained lichen which covered the uncrumbled surface of rock with its rough scales.

Mr. Hillbury was in search of a prospect hole, described as the highest one within a day's ride of the camp, where certain fossil records of the " Old Silurian " had lately come to light. By the measured clink of steel upon steel, they were evidently not far from some form of human labor. Following the trend of the mountain, they came upon two men standing face to face on a limestone ledge, at work upon it with hammer and drill. Fragments of broken rock and materials for blasting were scattered about. There was no shelter or sign of habitation near them. Josephine, looking back to speak to Mrs. Craig, saw that she had dismounted some distance below, and was seated on the sloping, rocky floor, while her husband readjusted her saddle-blanket. Presently he sat down beside her, leaving the horses fastened together by their bridles.

"Aren't they coming?" Josephine asked Mr. Hillbury.

"*Oh*, Craig!" he called; "are you coming up?"

"No," was the reply. "Take your time; we're all right."

They looked as if they were. Mrs. Craig, waving her hand to Josephine, stretched herself out flat upon the rock. Mr. Craig doubled his legs under him and lit a cigarette. Josephine looked rather wistfully at this comfortable pantomime.

"Aren't you tired yourself?" Bodewin asked.

"A little," she admitted. "How far is it to the lake?"

"Half an hour's climb down again. Let me take you off. It's a pity to get too tired on your first climb."

She let herself be lifted down. Bodewin hung her bridle over the pommel of his own saddle, and took his place beside her on the sun-warmed rock. Mr. Hillbury was already fossil-hunting, tapping about with his scientific hammer, while the dead home-strokes of the miner's sledge beat continuously on the silence. For the sake of a brief respite from the sound, Bodewin addressed one of the miners; stretching himself forward on his elbow to examine a hole they had prepared for blasting, he asked:

"Can you get enough powder in a hole of that size for such hard rock?"

"Eh?" The man who was striking the drill stopped, and the big sunburnt Irishman who held it replied:

"That's what I'm tellin' him," indicating his partner. "It's losin' our labor we are! Ye'll blaw and blaw and ye'll not get the fill o' yer hat! Thim drills is too short. What's *he* afther?" he asked, leaning upon his drill, and nodding his head with a confidential smile towards Mr. Hillbury.

"Prospecting for fossils," Bodewin replied.

"Is it one o' thim stawne bot'nists he is?"

Bodewin nodded. "Something like that."

"Sure, this is the place for 'im. There's plenty of it here."

He came down the ledge towards them, using his tool as a staff, and ringing it on the rock with each heavy, limping step. His partner remained above sitting on the heels of his boots, his elbows on his knees, his hands dropped between them holding his idle hammer. He was a slenderly built youth of about twenty, beardless, tanned to the color of a Mexican, with thin, rather handsome features, and a dull, passionate expression. He watched Josephine and Bodewin with listless attentiveness.

"What have you got here?" Bodewin inquired of the man with the drill, picking up some pieces of rock as he spoke.

"Well-le, there's galeny in it, and there's carbónnets," he replied, turning over the fragments of stone with his big, freckled, hairy hand. His manner lacked the enthusiasm of the typical miner, but he spoke with a degree of respect for his own prospects.

"Where are your carbonates?" Bodewin asked.

"And what d'ye call thim?" exhibiting a piece of rock the color of an over-burnt brick.

"There are no carbonates here." Bodewin spoke with reckless candor. "That reddish stuff is the oxide of iron."

"To the divvle wid yer ox-ides! I'll lay me ould hat that's the color we're lookin' for. Is it'n assayer ye are?"

"Take it over to the stone botanist and see what he makes of it," said Bodewin lazily.

"No, but is it an assay —"

"Take it to the botanist! He'll assay it for you."

"He is *lame!*" Josephine said, looking after him as he limped away over the rocks with his specimen in one hand and his drill in the other.

"Oh, no, he isn't; it's the national walk. Don't you see he is lame in both feet?"

"Weren't you rather cruel to him about his 'carbónnets'?"

"Not half as cruel as I am to Hillbury," Bodewin replied, laughing. "Hillbury would keep us here till night if something weren't sent to irritate him." Seeing that she still looked sorrowfully after the unlucky prospector, he added, "Would it be cruel to tell the camel he couldn't get through the needle's eye?"

"Is it as hopeless as that? Poor fellow! he will lose his labor, as he said."

"He will do well if he loses no more than his labor. They are a queer pair. What fate do you suppose sent a good-natured Irish bricklayer up here nearly to the top of Sheridan, silver hunting, with a Canadian half-breed, I should say by the looks of him," glancing upward toward the slim dark figure on the rocks above, "for a partner?"

"Where do you suppose they live?"

"They have a bough shanty, probably, in the nearest timber. Micky, I dare say, has a wife down in the camp, taking in washing to feed the kids, while he plays it alone up here for higher stakes."

Bodewin lay stretched out upon the rock in one of his camp-fire attitudes. Josephine, sitting a little above him, could see only the narrowing lines of the lower part of his face below his hat-brim. They were sensitive lines, and looked capable of much refinement of expression, but they rested habitually in a quietness that was like a mask. Dizzily and dreamily Josephine looked about her. She felt rather than saw how far they were exalted into that vast dome of light; what a little ledge of the world they rested on. The sun that beat upon the rock filled her veins with its potent warmth. It was like an exquisitely gentle and prolonged stream of electricity, suffusing the brain and penetrating the very tissues of the bones. It was intoxicating. Dark spots crossed her vision. She drew a long sigh of retarded breath and closed her eyes. Then she heard Bodewin speaking.

"Miss Newbold, I think after all you must let me answer that question."

Josephine waited a moment before replying. She felt it would be paltry to ask what question. She merely said: —

"Please let it be as if I had not asked it."

"How is that to be done?" Bodewin moved a a little so he could look up at her as she sat above him.

"May not one repent of a hasty speech, and withdraw it?"

"If there be any occasion for repentance. But it is not easy to forget words sincerely spoken. I think your question was a sincere one, Miss Newbold."

"What would it be if it were not that?" Josephine asked.

"It would not be worth remembering. But I have remembered it, you see, in spite of myself, I may say. I believe I agreed with you when you said you had no right to ask it. That was a hasty admission on my part."

"Not at all! You could not help seeing it was a blunder. I hoped you would have seen how sorry I was, and have had the grace to forget it."

Bodewin, feeling about among the loose fragments of rock under his hand, chose one and skipped it downward, watching it glinting along on its precipitious course until it vanished in the purple depth of shadow below them.

"Grant that it was a blunder," he resumed, "I think you do not often blunder in that way. There must have been some force of feeling behind the speech that you so deprecate. It could hardly have come from your lips merely." He looked at her and smiled. "We are in for it now, you see."

She did not return the smile. "I don't know what you mean by 'in for it.' There *is* no question. I have withdrawn it. It doesn't exist."

"You have a very lofty little way of annihilating the past; unfortunately, it doesn't affect my past. The question still exists for me. It has been existing steadily and waxing troublesome ever since I saw you."

"Oh!" said Josephine, with a sigh of impatience.

"Well, then, why did you ask it, Miss Newbold? You charged me the other evening with being a renegade to justice. Is it not so?"

Josephine opened her lips to protest, but saw the hopelessness of it, apparently, and preserved her silence of sufferance. Bodewin smiled again quietly:—

"It is not often a woman is called to plead for justice in opposition to sentiment — for my answer to your question must be in the name of something I shall have to call sentiment for want of a better word. You see what an unusual opportunity you have given me. It should be made a precedent, — if only I were worthy of my rôle." He jerked another pebble from his fingers into the abyss, and again he looked with a half-fascinated, half-teasing smile into the girl's troubled face.

"When will you hear my poor defence? There is not time to offer it now; besides, I should like to get up my case a little before presenting it."

Josephine would not speak. She felt how hot and flushed her cheeks were, and how her lips trembled in spite of herself.

"You will not be cruel enough to go away and leave the ghost of that unanswered question haunting me. I shall hear you all the way from Kansas City, saying, 'If you care for justice, why won't you — '"

"Will you please not repeat my words?" she interrupted, haughtily.

There was not a trace of mockery in his voice when he spoke again.

"They are not your words. You have parted with them; they have a life of their own now. Not if you live a thousand years will you ever get them back again."

She turned her full face towards him with a speechless, startled movement.

"You cannot separate a vital question from its answer," he continued. "You know that every now and then in the life of a nation or of a man the time comes for somebody to ask a question. The person who asks it may not wish to be the one chosen; but once the word is out it cannot rest until it gets itself answered, if it is a real question, even if it takes the nation's life, or the man's, to answer it. I have not deliberately thought about your question, Miss Newbold, but it is no exaggeration to say that since I saw you last I have thought of but little else. If I cannot answer it to your satisfaction, you may summon me to the trial as your witness."

"Answer it to yourself," she said, "and if truth and justice do not summon you, you have no right to be there."

"There are other obligations besides those of truth and justice."

"But I think those must come first."

"Now you touch upon the reason why I wish to lay my little problem before you. I had decided in favor of certain other obligations; I dare say I have become morbid about them. Because of your untroubled preference for truth and justice, and because you are a stranger, unbiased, as a wise young judge should be, I desire to set my small difficulty before you. I am tired of it. My conscience, when I question it, gives out only indistinct mutterings."

"You ask far too much of me. I cannot do this for you, Mr. Bodewin. I am not untroubled. I am not unbiased. I was thinking of my father. When I spoke to you I feared you might be refusing to testify because you knew of some reason, unknown to him or to Mr. Craig, why he ought not to win his suit. It was, of course, my own misgiving entirely. I have never mentioned it to any one, but it seemed to me a terrible thing that you should be willing to stand aside and see an honest man commit an unintentional fraud."

"But I told you I believed your father's side was the right side, did I not?"

"Yes, and I was satisfied."

"Then, once more, please, why did you ask me that question?"

"Why did I — what?" said Josephine confus-
edly.

"It was after I gave you, unconsciously enough,
that satisfaction you speak of, that you said, — well,
you will not let me repeat the words. Was there
not another misgiving? Has that been satisfied?"

"No," said Josephine, helplessly, "but it does
not concern — me."

"Whom does it concern, may I ask?"

"I am not so anxious to answer questions as
you are."

"Does it concern *me*, Miss Newbold? I seem
to be flattering myself, but there are not so many
parties in this affair. I can hardly suppose it is
Mr. Harkins you — "

"I know I have brought this on myself," cried
Josephine in desperate annoyance, "but don't you
think it has gone far enough now?"

"As soon as you have promised to give me an
opportunity to reply to whatever doubt prompted
your question, it will have gone far enough — not
till then."

"I have said that it does not concern me, and
have asked your pardon for letting you know I
had the doubt, or for having it, if you like. Can
I do more?"

" You have not said that your suspicions do not concern *me*."

" Suspicions ! "

" We will go back to the original word then — your question. Say that your question did not concern me, and I will not insist upon answering it."

Josephine was silent.

" You have called me to account for a course of action I am at perfect liberty to take and which no man has yet questioned. Is it quite just for you to refuse to hear my defence, such as it is? I don't claim it is sufficient."

" I will hear it."

" When, please ? "

" Whenever you like. But I cannot attempt to influence your decision. I would not do it if you were my own brother."

" It would be much less easy for you to, if I were. Does it seem to you too intimate a thing for me to ask of you ? "

" Yes, it does ! " she exclaimed eagerly — " precisely that ! "

" I don't regard it so, and I promise you I will not take advantage of it as an approach to anything of the sort in the future. For that matter, 'our acquaintance has no future any more than it has a past. It shares the spirit of this place, where we all live and live fast in the present, and then separate and know each other no more. I should like to believe that some instinct of helpfulness in you prompted those words which you regret, because they were unconventional. Don't regret them. Don't take back your words, but be true to them, and be brave enough not to shirk the sequel to them. The sequel to a question is its answer."

Josephine was far more startled by his earnestness than she had been chagrined by his badinage.

"Oh!" she cried in desperation, "why will you insist upon enforcing the sequel to such a foolish beginning? Why not let it rest? What is it but a trifle — a few poor words?"

"It is not a trifle to me, coming from you, if you please. It amounts to an accusation. It cannot be withdrawn to my satisfaction until it has been answered."

"I will listen to your answer, but more than that I insist you must not ask of me. I am not an expert on matters of the conscience — and I am being slowly consumed on this rock," she sighed.

"Forgive me!" he said, springing to his feet and holding out a hand to help her to rise. "Have I made you hate me?"

"Yes!" she declared. "Do not put your problem in my hands. I am as biased as the most disagreeable half-hour I ever spent in my life can make me!"

"I am sorry you should be indebted to me for it."

"Oh, I am not! I am indebted to myself. But I shall hate you for it, just the same."

"I have no doubt of it. I ought to be proud to suffer vicariously when I can save you from yourself by doing so. You must be very severe with yourself when you are fairly roused."

"I think I have never been fairly roused."

"If you will pardon the conjunction, I think we neither of us have," he said.

"It must be a horrible experience to be utterly and fundamentally hateful to one's self."

"I think it is an experience that comes to but few, and not to those who most need it. Here comes Hillbury! He seems to have torn himself from the bosom of the Old Silurian at last."

As Bodewin put Josephine on her saddle again, he said to her, " Whatever it was you accused me of in your own thoughts, let it rest until I can talk with you again."

" 'Still harping,' " she replied, and hurried after Mr. Hillbury, who had mounted and ridden on to join the Craigs. Bodewin followed musingly, and did not attempt to lessen the distance between them.

CHAPTER VII.

MR. CRAIG GOES A-HUNTING.

THE lake, when they had reached it, was, after all, in size hardly more than a large pond. It was on the edge of the timber, a clear, still eye of water, darkly bordered by pine-trees, with one bright spot of reflected blue shining in the middle, like an immeasurable far-off sky in the depths of the lake. They dismounted again and spread out their lunch in the dappled shade. It was not an hilarious picnic. Mrs. Craig and Josephine were both tired. The latter was also dazed with her long discussion on the rocks in the blinding sunlight. Bodewin, she thought, must be of the salamander species, since he was so sluggish in the shade and woke to such a burst of argumentative energy in the glare of the sun. He ate little and talked less, relapsing into the background of conversation, as his wont was when it became general.

When the sylvan meal was over, Mr. Craig

unslung his shot-gun from his saddle and clambered down into the heavier timber, in search of wood-pigeons, he said, an object which excited the derision of the other men of the party. Bodewin referred to the "man in the wilderness," and asked Mrs. Craig, as an authority on nursery rhymes, to quote for him : —

> "The man in the wilderness asked me
> How many strawberries grew in the sea.
> I answered him as I thought good —
> As many as red-herrings grow in the wood."

"What are you laughing at ? — because he goes to the wood for wood-pigeons ?" asked Mrs. Craig.

"To this particular wood," said Hillbury. "You would not laugh at a man for going to the sea for fish; but if he were much of a fisherman, he would hardly go to Baffin's Bay for mullet."

"Oh, you are all so technical," said Mrs. Craig; "for my part I think a little vague general information is much more restful."

They sat under the low spruce boughs by the lake, talking and listening in the rustle of the deep tideless water and the sur-r-r-ing of the wind in the trees. Mr. Hillbury produced his fossils, delicate forms of earliest organic life imprinted in glistening pyrites on the dark Silurian slate.

The ladies held the fragments of the old sea-beach on the palms of their hands, and examined them with a magnifying glass, exclaiming over them in their soft staccato. Once there came from the wood the sound of a single shot. Bodewin and Hillbury both recognized it as the note of Craig's gun.

"He has found the wood-pigeon!"

They waited for a second shot, but none came. When the slanting sunbeams had pierced their covert, they abandoned it, and strolled along the shore of the lake. Mr. Hillbury walked with Josephine, pointing out to her the long formless ridges which marked the recession of one of those vast glacial seas that had crawled down the mountain-sides during the epoch of ice. The lake had been formed between two of these ancient moraines. Solitary, unvisited, bare of human association or tradition as it was, — "foster-child of silence and slow time," — its cradled waters were uncounted centuries old before the story of man began.

Bodewin jeered at his friend a little for his popular science, and was rebuked by Mrs. Craig. She had herself more than once interrupted Mr. Hillbury, and asked for a moment's silence, during which she seemed to listen for sounds from the wood.

The afternoon wore away. The sun dropped below the western ridge and left the lake gray in shadow. Since the single report of his gun, nothing had been heard from Craig. His wife could no longer conceal her wretchedness at his absence. She sat, pale and silent, looking from one to the other, while Bodewin and Hillbury persistently made light of it, meanwhile planning a search for him on the excuse that it was already late for their homeward start. The pleasure party had reached a pitch of positive demoralization, as far as the women were concerned, when Craig himself was heard shouting from the opposite shore of the lake. He was walking fast under the trees, apparently none the worse for the gun which he carried over his shoulder. Mrs. Craig was a little overcome at the sight of him, and laughed in a nervous, immoderate way at her late fears; but she recovered herself when Craig arrived, red and out of breath with his hurried walk around the lake, and received him with lively upbraidings. He was unnecessarily cheerful, and he had besides an important air of adventure about him which, under the circumstances, called for immediate snubbing. When he had been brought to a proper sense of his weakness and evil behavior, he was allowed to tell his story.

"But first, where is the wood-pigeon?" said Hillbury.

"Oh, I found her, but I didn't bring her home!" Craig did not mind confessing, he said, that he had missed his bearings. "One part of the wood looked so confoundedly like another, and there was no wind."

"No *wind!*" his wife interrupted.

"Not in the timber — not a breath — and mighty little sun. You are higher up, remember. You had an hour's more sun than I had. I began to think I had been walking about long enough without getting anywhere, when I heard a horse whinny. A few steps on I came to a corral, and just beyond it a biggish log-cabin. The back end of it ran butt into the dump of an old prospect hole. The ground rose suddenly behind the cabin, and the dump sloped up against the hill. There was a long bench by the door, and there sat the prettiest girl, in a calico dress, with her arms bare, feeding a setter-pup! She had him in her lap, and he was nuzzling about in a saucer of

milk she held, and sometimes licking her arms by
mistake. She had one of those low Greek heads
my wife likes so much, with small intelligence in
it, I should say, but plenty of hair on it — yellow
hair, braided in two tails and wound around the
head. I asked her the way to the lake. She
stared at me and said she didn't know of any
lake; she hadn't been in these parts long. She
had a kind of sweet, stolid way that was uncommonly taking in connection with her looks. I
wanted to look at her a little longer, so I asked
her if the pup was for sale."

Mr. Craig was here interrupted in his narrative
by laughter and applause.

"She said that she didn't know. Her father
wasn't home. I might call again and inquire. I
asked her when I would be likely to find her
father at home in case I called. She couldn't tell.
Her father was mostly home except when he
went to the camp, or over the range to a prospect he had there.

"I asked permission to climb up the dump and
see if I could get a better view of my surroundings from the top of it. She gave me permission
and followed me up there with the pup in her
arms. There was just a streak of sunlight left.

It touched her hair very prettily, and it showed me which way was west, and so I made for the lake and left her there, making no end of a pretty picture of herself with the sun on her golden hair."

> " The man in the wilderness asked me
> How many strawberries grew in the sea.
> I answered him as I thought good —
> As many as pretty girls grow in the wood,"

laughed Mrs. Craig.

"Come, 'saddle up, saddle !'" said Bodewin. "We won't get out of the woods now before dark !"

Mr. Newbold had ordered a supper for the party on their return. Mrs. Craig excused herself on her children's account from remaining to it. Craig, as he rode away beside his wife, called back to Hillbury:

"The next time you go up the lake way, look up my cabin in the timber, will you? I'll commission you to get me that setter-pup."

" I don't see how you can stand so much of Craig," said Bodewin, crossly.

" Craig is a good fellow."

" A good fellow, yes — and a common fellow. It makes me sick to see him ride."

"He rides well enough," said Hillbury. "The fact is, there isn't one man in a hundred one wants to spend a whole day in the woods with."

"As for that cabin and girl and pup story," Bodewin went on.

"Don't you believe it?" asked Hillbury.

"Hardly. I am tolerably well acquainted with those woods myself. He got himself lost, like the tender-foot he is, and invented this story to carry it off. That sunlight-on-her-yellow-hair business is rather too musty."

"I think you are mistaken, Bodewin. Craig to me looked and talked like a man who had just had that sort of luck, to be stumbling along disgustedly and suddenly come upon the little idyl in the forest. If it were an invention, why put in the old prospect hole and the setter-pup?"

"It is possible he has seen such a cabin and such a group by the door, but I doubt if he saw them this afternoon."

"Bodewin, I will bet you a box of cigars I will find that cabin myself within a week."

"You'll waste your time and lose your cigars, — and Craig is an ass!"

They were in the office of the Wiltsie House, sitting on the row of chairs along the wall opposite the clerk's desk. In the confusion of un-modulated voices their own lower tones were lost.

"How long would you be a friend of Mrs. Craig if she knew you thought so?" Hillbury asked.

"I am not indebted to Craig for his wife's ac-quaintance. I knew Mrs. Craig years before he ever saw her. At a pinch I dare say she could exist without me, and I possibly without her. There are times when I find Craig too great a discount on the friendship of any woman."

"What is the matter with you, old man?"

"Hillbury," said Bodewin, with a sudden change of manner, taking a small, worn, leather note-book from his pocket, and turning over its pages absently, "I wish the Lord would let me burn this book! I have dropped it down shafts; I have left it in my old coat-pockets when I moved camp, and had it sent back to me; I have, within the past year, taken it out more than once with as deliberate intention as I have of going to bed to-night of destroying it. Upon my soul I can't do it!"

"What have you in it?"

"Well, amongst other things, some memoranda

relating to the Harkins and Eagle Bird suit. The Eagle Bird people want me to appear on their side."

"So I have heard," Hillbury said, much interested, and quietly observant of his friend. He had speculated not a little upon the probable meaning of Bodewin's reluctance to testify on this suit, even as he often speculated about Bodewin himself; but the two men might have been the sole occupants of a lighthouse for a year without its once occurring to Hillbury to ask his friend the question Miss Newbold had posed him with an hour after his introduction to her.

"Yes," Bodewin continued. "It's a horrible nuisance. I would like to tell you about it, but you know me too well, Hillbury. I should hate to have the thing perpetually associated with me in your mind. The only people, after all, to confide in, are those whom you like at first sight, and never expect to see again."

"I don't agree with you, but then that's nothing new."

"I will tell you this much," Bodewin began, but Hillbury interrupted.

"Why tell me anything if you don't wish to tell me all? Half confidences are so often misleading."

" Because it bores me so!   Hillbury, I am sold
into bondage! I am under an obligation to Harkins, — a most delicate, personal, strenuous obligation. It is a thousand times worse than if
he had saved my life.   It involves —"   Bodewin
found he had been precipitate after all.   He could
not say to Hillbury, whose people in the East
knew his own, " It involves my sister's name and
memory."   He paused, with his friend's dark,
grave eyes resting on his face, and ended stupidly.
" It involves the name of a woman — one of the
sweetest God ever made for man to destroy.   If I
have to balk Harkins's game, he is just clever
enough to see that here is his revenge.   Don't I
know with what an unholy glee he would parade
my obligation to him and his generosity to her
whose name I must protect? "

" Bodewin, my dear fellow, will you forgive me
for saying this whole thing, as you hint at it,
sounds to me fantastic and morbid.   I have
always suspected you of a dangerous kind of
enthusiasm in your moral processes.   The business of living is, after all, nothing but a series of
investments at a high rate of interest with corresponding risks, or at a low rate with good security.   I am afraid you go in too much for the

ten per cents and the risks in your moral investments."

"What do you mean by the risks?"

"You can't need to be told what they are. You'd
better stick to the plain lines of duty, so far as
Harkins is concerned, and protect your own name
first. It occurs to you, no doubt, that this is a
little gratuitous on my part; but I am older than
you, and on some points not so sensitive."

"Not so vulnerable, you mean," said Bodewin,
with a touch of bitterness.

Hillbury had no time to respond before Mr.
Newbold joined them with his daughter's excuses
instead of her company. "She was tired," he
said, "and did not care to change her dress. She'd
have come down fast enough if Mrs. Craig had
stayed, but she's not accustomed to be the only
lady; and the restaurant, you know, at this
hour — "

The green-baize-covered door closed upon the
sentence.

CHAPTER VIII.

BODEWIN'S SISTER.

BODEWIN belonged to that generation of the country's youth which was hurried into premature manhood by the shock of the civil war. He was sixteen the spring of 1861, when his elder brother left home in response to the President's call for volunteers. That summer young Bodewin went up to Yale to pass his preliminary examination. He was already a man in stature, and it was thought the best way to keep him from haunting the recruiting offices. The second year closed darkly, with Burnside's losses before Fredericksburg, which increased the demoralization of the Army of the Potomac, on which the hopes of the East were fixed. Bodewin entered with all the passionate pessimism of youth, debarred from action, into the uncertainties of the situation. If disruption were at hand, he did not care for his future: if the war were to be successfully and honorably brought to a close, he could not accept it at the price of some better man's life. Thus he brooded, sitting on the college fence, under the budding elms, in the sad spring twilights.

He wrote to his brother for advice. Captain Bodewin told him plainly that his place was with the non-combatants for at least four years to come, and reminded him that in all wars, in all ages, the widow has ever been entitled to one son. This was not the advice young Bodewin wanted. In the face of it he abandoned his books and followed his boyish leadings into the army, enlisting as a private in his brother's regiment, the —— Connecticut Cavalry. He served faithfully, but without distinction, until the close of the war. When the armies were disbanded he went home alone, an old-looking boy of twenty, already acquainted with grief, lean of cheek and limb, with hollows under his young eyes, with a habit of silence, with the discipline of ten years crowded into two — a discipline with stern limitations, however. He had learned something of endurance, of obedience, and of self-restraint; but of the world of men and women he had been spared to spend his life among, he had all to learn.

The house had lost its mainstay — that wise elder

brother, whom the mother believed Heaven had given her to be the support of her widowed years. He had fallen in the last great charge of the war. His loss was embittered to Bodewin by a sense of its needlessness, for the struggle was virtually over. It seemed as if the lives lost that day were but heaped upon the over-full measure of the nation's dead, in the very wantonness of sacrifice.

The night after the battle Bodewin searched the field for his brother's body. A comrade kept at his side, and helped him in his last poor services to the dead. The young men were of the same regiment; each had seen and approved the other in action, but beyond this they scarcely knew each other's names. As they stood together by the new-made grave, in the white dawn before sunrise, Bodewin had said to his comrade : —

" My mother must thank you for this night's work."

They parted with a promise from Lieutenant Eustis that he would visit Bodewin at the latter's home if both lived to see the end of the war.

Eustis had accepted the invitation with some diffidence.

" You must not ask me under an impression

that I was a friend of your brother's," he had
said. "I admired him greatly, but I am bound to
confess that, so far as I know, the feeling was not
mutual."

Bodewin could not have known that this scrupulousness was far from being characteristic of
Frank Eustis. It was a genuine touch of candor
and humility won from him by the circumstances
which had brought the two young men together;
but it was misleading, as only nature can be.

Bodewin took up the responsibilities death had
laid on him in a condition of mind and body calculated to breed morbid views of duty. He was
physically relaxed by the reaction which followed
the change from army life to the life of home.
The heaviness of his first sorrow was upon him.
There was, besides, the dawn of another sorrow
he could not blind himself to. It could hardly
be called a change in his mother; a lapse, rather,
of the powers mental as well as physical — the
mark left by the war on a gentle nature, strong
only in its affections. The heart of the family
she would be, ever. Its head she had ceased to
be.

Bodewin resigned his hopes of a profession,
and applied himself to the resuscitation of his

mother's property. His father had for fifteen years held a professorship in an Eastern college. Late in life he had married the only surviving child and heiress of Simeon Wills, a member of the Society of Friends, and a well-to-do farmer, who had widened his landmarks on the Sound shore of Connecticut until they included about three hundred acres of salt-marsh, sea-beach, woodland, and stony pasture. To their grandfather's house Tristram Bodewin's widow had taken her children after her husband's death, and since that time, early in their childish recollections, they had known no other home.

True to her father's faith herself, she had not tried to make proselytes even of her own children, but to each one in different degrees she had transmitted that quiet persistence which was one of her own least conspicuous but most inherent traits.

Bodewin had left his sister a child. A child she still seemed to him, although she was tall for sixteen, when to the broken household came Eustis in his faded cavalry uniform, with his record of fifty battles and that last service of his to the dead son of the house to aid him in making an impression. Ellen Bodewin was not a beauty, but in many ways she was beautiful. In after years, when the thought of his sister had become the permanent ache of his heart, Bodewin always saw her as he used to see her that summer, crossing the grass at twilight in her white dress and black ribbons, her profile distinct, almost luminous in its fairness, against the mass of dark-green shrubbery.

Bodewin spent many hours that summer at the black, pigeon-holed "secretary" in the dining-room, employed in a retrospect of accounts which invariably closed with the balance on the wrong side. The short, warm evenings he spent with his mother, in the unlighted parlor, where she lay on her sofa in the exhaustion of spent and tear-less grief. In those silent sessions with their dead, mother and son alike felt that the child of the house should have no part. Her share in the family sorrow had been less, as her knowledge of her brother was less than theirs; and her age was not ripe for sorrow. Yet they would have keenly resented any outside suggestion that Ellen took their great and common loss not sufficiently to heart.

Eustis came for a week the first time. He spoke of business engagements in New York.

Bodewin found him there a month later, looking haggard and seedy. An old wound he had carried since Fredericksburg had been troubling him, he said. His family were in Genoa, where his father held a consulship. Bodewin asked him to come to Cranberry Beach for another fortnight, and incidentally lent him a little money. Again Eustis and Ellen were together, and in the still midsummer weather another tragedy of the war was hurrying to its consummation.

On the edge of the lawn where it sloped toward the pied salt marshes, there was a granite bowlder, cool, deeply bedded in ferns, and shaded by a clump of maple trees. A breeze from the blue water beyond the marshes was always blowing in their tops. On the hottest days, when the close-sheltered house dozed in the sun, Eustis, with the chess-board and the hammock-cushions under his arm, followed by Ellen shading her forehead with the latest magazine, crossed the dry, scintillating grass to this island of coolness and shadow. They were as secluded here, with the fields of heat making a wide stillness around them, as Ferdinand and Miranda in the island cave.

There were sandy paths through the scrub oak and barberry bushes leading to the shore, and there was a shallow river winding through the marshes, down which they drifted, sitting face to face but seldom speaking. All these landways and waterways they had taken together before the fortnight was over. They led all in the same direction, and ended in the catastrophe of a young girl's life.

In those days men were worshipped because they were soldiers merely. They needed no other attribute, and Eustis possessed several others beside that perilous association with a brother's memory. When after the second visit Bodewin heard his mother ask Eustis to come to them again at Christmas, if his family were still abroad, it occurred to him at last that they were seeing a good deal of their summer guest. On his next visit to New York he took pains to make some inquiries about Eustis. It was like going to a shelf piled with rubbish and pulling at a corner of the lowest object of the heap. He found a clew to one shabby little affair in looking up Eustis's antecedents, and the rest came tumbling about his ears. It was sickening, but it was a necessary lesson for the protector of a family of women to learn, and Bodewin congratulated himself on having learned it in good season. He was alone with his mother in the dining-room on the evening of his return. It was now late in October, and the evenings were cool. The blaze of a few sticks on the hearth was the only light in the room, while the open door showed a broad patch of moonlight on the hall floor, squared with the shadow of the window sash. Bodewin told his mother all that seemed necessary of his discoveries in regard to Eustis.

"He must not come at Christmas, or at any other time," he concluded.

Mrs. Bodewin seemed troubled beyond a reasonable conception of any feeling she could possibly have in the matter. Did he wish the acquaintance to cease? she asked her son.

"On the part of the women of the family, yes," he replied.

She reminded him of the family obligation. He assured her he would take care of that. In the greatest agitation she begged him to be careful what he said, for his sister's sake.

"What has Eustis to do with my sister?" Bodewin inquired, and then the blow came. Eustis had asked Ellen to be his wife. She loved him, and was waiting only for the consent of her mother and brother. The mother had already given hers.   Ellen had been receiving letters from Eustis since his last visit.   Mrs. Bodewin had felt obliged to speak to her about them.   She had first done so during Bodewin's absence, and had then received her child's confession.

Eustis had offered himself to her before his departure.   She had not permitted him to speak to her family then, because the time had seemed unfit.

"She was not ashamed to do the thing she was ashamed to speak of!" Bodewin burst out passionately.

"She is but a child!   What else can she be?" the mother pleaded.   "And she has not answered his letters or given him her promise except on conditions."

"Eustis is not the man for her to be making conditions with, mother! If she is a child, she must be treated like one.   She must be prevented from doing herself this injury."

"It is done, it is done!" the mother wailed, "and we have done it.   It lies at our door."

"It lies at my door!" said Bodewin.   "Mother, I no more imagined any danger to Ellen in his being here than to you. How was I to know a girl is like that?   To be won in a week, in a month, by the first man who looks at her!   To be thinking of a lover, with her brother not six months in his grave!"

"Hush!" his mother said, rising and pointing towards the door as she faltered towards him. He turned and confronted his sister. She had heard his words distinctly in the quiet house as she came down the stairs from her chamber. What influence Bodewin might have gained over her, when his revolt against the pang of self-conviction cooled, had she never heard those wild words, may be questioned. As it was, the insult had struck too deep for explanation or retraction. There was, perhaps, enough of truth in the words to make them unforgivable. Bodewin patiently went over the charges against Eustis with his mother, and in turn she endeavored to set them before Ellen. The effect they produced was one of repulsion, not towards the accused, but the accuser. She was prepared for prejudice in one by whom she had herself been misjudged, and the seeds of counsel fell upon stony ground. There were long, heart-breaking arguments between mother and daughter, and hopeless consultations between mother and son. But the brother and sister were no longer on terms of argument or consultation, still less of entreaty.

The struggle ended as it must always end between young love and old decrees. It was a relief at last when the marriage took place, two years later. Ellen's position had come to be that of a martyr persecuted by her brother for her faithfulness to her lover; for the mother had not been able to keep a consistent attitude of protest, and long before the marriage took place had offered but a passive resistance. Her losses had weakened her power of enduring the pain of those she loved. The risks of Ellen's marriage were in the future, while the sight of her unhappiness was an ever-present torture. Nor was it possible for a woman with Mrs. Bodewin's experience of men and of marriage to conceive what those risks were likely to be with one like Eustis. She had no real conception of Eustis himself, — a man who could not be relied upon even in the direction of his weaknesses, for with a fatal inconsistency he had not been weak in his pursuit of Ellen. He had been as true to his purpose as if the truth were in him.

According to his weakness and her strength he no doubt loved her, and the purest sentiment of his life kept him at his highest level during the months of his probation. There were times when

Bodewin was ready to believe that it was he who was the victim of hallucination, and that Ellen's case was indeed one of persecution, so filled was the house with that sense of her outraged love which her mute presence conveyed. But on the day of her marriage, in that searching light in which love, acknowledged and triumphant, exhibits itself, Bodewin saw that he was not mistaken. In certain sure and subtle ways he felt that the bridegroom was hopelessly beneath the dignity of his part. It could only be a question of time.

It was now thirteen years since the day of his sister's marriage, and during ten of those years Bodewin had held himself ready for the time when she would need him. His life had been ordered solely with reference to that time and that atonement he believed he would be permitted to make his sister for the husband he had given her and the father he had given her children. He thought no more of marriage for himself than if his mother and sister had been the only women in the world. He felt that his sister held a mortgage on his life, and year by year the unpaid interest went to swell the debt.

Eustis took his young wife to Virginia City, where he began his business career as a broker in mines and real estate. In the course of a year or two he had joined that wandering community which follows the changes of luck from one mining camp to another.

Bodewin made mines his business also, in a different way, partly that he might not lose sight of his sister on her unblest pilgrimage, partly because the event had proved that he was no farmer, and he needed to put money in his purse for the time when his sister would accept his atonement. The mother still lived at Cranberry Beach, in the retirement that suited her health and circumstances, with an unmarried sister as her companion. Those lapses of memory which had first warned Bodewin of the break in his mother's strength were now her greatest mercy.

Ellen seldom wrote, never unless in times of comparative prosperity; and as these grew more and more infrequent, the letters came at longer and longer intervals. They knew that children were born to her, and that she had lost children, but of the nameless humiliations of her life, of the eddy of shabby cares in which it went round and round, wearing into her soul, they could but silently conjecture; and as one prophecy after another of all those that had been made concerning her marriage fulfilled itself, she wrapped herself more and more closely in the fate she had chosen, and hid her wounds with a pride that seemed all that was left of her love for her brother. The loving can never understand those who have ceased to love; and as little as he could comprehend the sundering of a life-tie like that between himself and the sister he had so innocently and hopelessly injured, still less could Bodewin fathom the mystery of a weak man's hold on the life of a strong woman, who holds forlornly to her own pure vow, as the sanctification of the shame it covers.

CHAPTER IX.

THE TENDER MERCIES OF THE WICKED.

One day, now three years gone, in the Mining Exchange in San Francisco, Bodewin took up a Deadwood paper, a week old by its date, and saw a notice of the death of Frank Eustis. His body had been found in the street, dead by his own hand; "probable cause, domestic anxieties and drink." The notice was headed, "Good-bye, Frank!" Bodewin learned more of the affair later in Deadwood, from Henry Wilkinson, a lawyer of his acquaintance, with whom Eustis had spoken last. Wilkinson had met Eustis about twelve o'clock the night of his death, as he himself was coming out of the Varieties Theatre with the crowd. Eustis was hurrying along through a light fall of snow, bareheaded and half wild with drink.

"For God's sake, Henry, lend me five dollars!" he had said. "I expect my wife and four children in by the stage to-morrow night, and I haven't so much as a roof to put over their heads."

"That wife-and-children game is about played, Frank," had been Wilkinson's reply. Eustis had been borrowing money for six months or more on the strength of the imminent arrival of his family.

"They are coming this time, by God! But they won't find me here!" were his last words as he ran on down the street, slipping and falling at last in the soft snow.

Wilkinson had pulled him up, set him on his feet, brushed the snow from his hair and neck, and, putting his own hat on his head, had left him staring stupidly before him.

He was found the next morning stiff and cold, with his head on the curb-stone and a bullet-hole in the side of it.

The night following that morning Ellen Eustis arrived with her children. There were but three. To the last Eustis had not been able to help lying a little in an unimportant way. His wife had come by stage, two hundred miles across the northern desert. She had waited, in the last poor refuge where he had left her, for Eustis to return or send for her. His letters spoke of his

success in the new camp, but there were no inclo-
sures of money and no summons for her to join
him and share his success. At last, when her
means of support were nearly exhausted, she had
taken what money remained to her and desperately followed her husband, to what end she knew
not, except that it could not be worse than the one
she had in view. The man who probably saved her
from dying on that journey was Colonel William
Harkins. As an experienced traveller, the Colonel
had secured for himself the entire back seat of
the coach, and with lunch-basket, rugs, seal-skin
coat, cigars, and paper novels, had expected to
make the trip across the frozen alkali plains in
comparative comfort.

It was just his luck, so he commiserated himself
as he surveyed his fellow-passengers, to find in
front of him, occupying the middle seat, a wan-
cheeked young mother with three pretty, thinly-
clad children, vis-à-vis with two Chinamen and a
Jew " drummer," riding on the forward seat.

The first day's ride was not half over before
Harkins had " borrowed " two of the children,
and was telling them stories and romping with
them, while the mother from time to time looked
back and smiled at the sound of their laughter.

When the boy grew sleepy he helped her to make
a bed for him on the seat beside her, and arranged
his travelling-bag under her feet, that she might
the more easily support the child's head in her
lap. At the squalid meal station he thrust her
into the warmest corner by the fire, and bribed,
from the meagre hospitality of the place, the best
it could furnish for her comfort. He led the way
back to the stage with the youngster on his shoulder, and, putting him into his mother's arms, begged her to keep his seat for him while he walked
on a mile or so for exercise. Not to be burdened
with it while walking, he threw off his fur coat
and asked permission to wrap her and the little
fellow in it, until he should need it again. For
the little fellow's sake she allowed him to do so.
Laughingly he cuddled the two little girls in his
rugs, and bidding them let no one into his seat
in his absence, trudged on ahead of the stage.
When it overtook him he climbed up beside the
driver and sat there smoking until it grew dusk.
Looking back into the coach, he saw that the
mother and children were asleep, snugly wrapped
in his rugs and furs. He called himself a d——
fool, took something to keep out the cold, and
crawling down into the boot under the driver's

blankets, slept there all night on the mail bags. The mother began the next day with an effort at independence, but was soon too much exhausted by the unavoidable hardships of the journey and her children's constant claims on her strength to resist the ingenious and persistent kindness of her fellow-traveller. The Colonel's luxuries were her necessities. He diverted them to her use with that understanding, cheerfully insisted on by him, and helplessly admitted by herself.

The stage office was buzzing with talk of the latest camp tragedy on the evening of the travellers' arrival.

"Oh, it is only some poor cuss got cleaned out at faro, and shot himself last night," Harkins replied to the young mother's inquiries, as she sat with her children around her in a corner of the crowded room. "What did you say your husband's first name was, Mrs. Eustis? — Frank? Well, see here! You'd better get a room here to-night. He didn't get your telegram most likely. I don't seem to see him anywheres about. We'll look him up first thing in the morning. Those children ought to have something to eat. I'll have something sent up to you. Now don't you worry, will you? You leave me to find your husband." So, talking rapidly, he hurried her away from the merciless gossip of the crowd, which suspended its words long enough to stare at poor Frank's widow as she passed out of the room.

Yes; it was just his luck — that the husband of his pretty, pale fellow-traveller should be the dead man whom the Masons were to bury to-morrow; that she should be nearing the time of her woman's utmost need, penniless, homeless, without a friend in the place. The next day he took her to a cabin in the outskirts of the town. It was her husband's house, he told her. This was the furniture Eustis had bought in preparation for her coming. These trifles of groceries and what not he had ordered in her husband's name; it was all the same. Evidently he had not been housekeeping himself and was a little hurried by her telegram. Then he *had* received it? — Where was he? What was he keeping from her? He met the question simply and squarely, cursing his luck again that there was no one but himself to meet it. He had occasion to call himself a fool with profane emphasis more than once that day, because he could not forget the new-made widow and her forlorn little brood. He mentioned her case to a lady friend of his, who promised to look after her should she need a woman's help. Harkins's lady friend was one of those who have lost all for themselves, yet still have something to give to another's distress.

Frank Eustis's wife had long ago learned how cruel are the tender mercies of the feebly wicked. It was only one more step in the long, downward path she had taken beside him, — the last step, — and it was characteristic of him that he had left her to take it alone.

It is a ten-days' journey, including the stage ride, from San Francisco to Deadwood, with the roads in good condition. The roads were at their worst, and Bodewin, starting immediately on the news of Eustis's death, was two weeks on the way. He reached Deadwood one evening about ten o'clock, bruised, supperless, and stiff with cold. The usual crowd was gathered in the bar-room of the North-western Hotel. It seemed as good a place as any to begin inquiries for his sister. He was sure to find some of Eustis's friends there. When Bodewin asked news of Eustis's wife there was a dead silence in the room. Colonel Harkins stepped out of the crowd, and taking Bodewin apart, asked: —

"Who might you be, inquiring for Frank Eustis's wife?"

"I am Mrs. Eustis's brother," Bodewin replied.

"The devil you are!" he remarked, in the same low, deliberate tone. "You're a sweet brother! Why didn't you get in here two weeks ago?"

Bodewin did not make the mistake of resenting this singular reception of a stranger. He was familiar enough with frontier manners to understand it as some rude form of championship of his sister, founded on his own· apparent or fancied neglect.

"Never mind about two weeks ago," he replied. "Do you know where my sister is now?"

Harkins looked him over again carefully before he spoke. "Better take a drink and eat something."

Bodewin declined to act on this suggestion, and showed some restiveness under Harkins's prolonged interest in him.

"Come on, then," the latter said, and led the way into the street. Walking fast, without speaking, they came to that low cabin in the thinly built part of the town where the widow had found shelter. Harkins knocked at the door softly, or so Bodewin fancied.

"Is my sister not well?" he asked.

"She is well," Harkins answered, solemnly, "since two o'clock last night."

He left Bodewin waiting at the door. After some delay it was opened by a white-faced, red-cheeked young woman, who stared at Bodewin, and looked as if she might have simpered a little if she had been less sleepy.

"Take a chair," she said. " Be you a friend of hers?" indicating with a motion of her hand the closed door of an adjoining room.

"I am her brother," Bodewin replied.

" You don't say! Where are you from?"

Bodewin mentioned the place.

" How long is it since you seen her?"

" Nearly ten years."

" Well, I declare! I guess she's changed some. D'you want to see her to-night? She ain't laid out yet. There wasn't anything of her own fit to put on her. She could 'a' worn a white silk of mine; it's some soiled, but it might 'a' done with lace over the front of the waist. But the Colonel wouldn't hear to it. He's having a splendid cashmere robe made for her."

Bodewin got up and went to the door. He leaned in the open doorway, with his face towards the cool night, while a faintness that had overcome him passed. He felt the woman's hand on his arm. "Here, drink this! You look like you was goin' to be sick." She held a tumbler half full of whiskey towards him. He asked for water and she dipped him a glassful from a pail beside the door.

"You'd better not see her to-night," the woman persisted, following him into the room again, "though she don't look bad. She ain't been sick long. Did you know there was a little baby? It's dead, too, poor thing! I expect *his* mother'll be glad it didn't live. There's enough of 'em to leave for other folks to take care of."

"Whose mother?" Bodewin asked, lifting his head to look at the speaker.

"Frank's mother. She's been sent for. Didn't you know?"

"Who sent for her?"

"The Colonel did."

"Will you tell me who is the Colonel?"

"Ain't you acquainted with Colonel Bill Harkins? It was lucky for Frank's wife *he* didn't stand on no ceremony. They rode in the same coach from the end of the track. Why, man, he done everything for her! Fed her and kep' her warm, and tended her young ones, and she not fit for travellin'. He's paid her way ever since she got in. This here house he's rented for her, and everything in it was bought with his money, though he never let her know it. You don't know the Colonel? Well, it's about time you did!"

"Will you let me see my sister?" Bodewin said, rising.

He was taken into the cold inner chamber, where on a clean white bed a sheet, smoothly spread, covered without concealing a motionless woman's form. There was the outline of the low pillowed head, the hands unstirred upon the breast, the small thin body sloping downwards, the little feet that propped the sheet scarcely higher than a child's. Bodewin knelt on the floor by the bedside, smitten hard and deep in every spot that anguish knows, — crushed, broken utterly. And the woman beside him — whom no one wept for, though she was more dead than death itself to all that makes a woman's life — hid with her thin hands the roses that stared on her white cheeks, and sobbed aloud.

Did she weep for herself only, as a child weeps at the sight of grief, or remembering that laughter and jests of men, nevermore men's despairing tenderness, and hopeless, hard-wrung tears, were her portion forever?

When he was alone with his dead, Bodewin folded down the sheet and looked at what lay beneath. He had known in part, and prophesied according to his knowledge, but he was in the presence now of that before which prophecies shall fail and tongues shall cease and knowledge shall vanish away. In the mercy of God it was well with her at last, and with the child that lay beside her in its long sleep that life had broken only for a few feeble breaths.

Bodewin would have found it impossible to escape from the details of his sister's last hours, had he wished to do so. They were in the mouths of strangers, who made them the medium of intercourse unsought by him and unspeakably harrowing. He knew, from various sources, the full extent of his indebtedness to Colonel Harkins, through his sister. The conjunction was torture to him. He tried in vain to get rid of the pecuniary part of the burden at the least, but the Colonel refused to overhaul his back accounts.

"It's all right," he repeated. "I haven't spent any money on her to hurt anybody, — nothing more than any man would do for a lady passenger."

The orphaned children had been taken home by a respectable matron of the neighborhood, whose offer of assistance had come too late to benefit the mother. The possibility had never occurred to Bodewin that his sister's children might be left to any one's care but his own, in case of their father's death or failure to provide for them. But, between the day of the funeral and that of Mrs. Eustis's arrival in the camp, he had time to think over his sister's last expressed wish, and to endeavor to reconcile himself to its provisions. She had chosen to leave her children to her husband's relations, ignoring her own blood. It was but the finishing touch to the devoted consistency of her wifehood. They were his children as well as hers; though by his life he had forfeited a father's right, in death she would not deprive him of a father's place in his children's memories. His own mother should exonerate him and atone for his shortcomings in the new generation that carries with it always the seed of the last one's blighted hopes.

Bodewin accepted his sister's decision, not without a forlorn pride in her steadfastness. But it left him objectless, purposeless, with his atonement on his hands. He had waited long, had kept the chambers of his heart empty and ready for the guest who had failed him at the last —who he now knew had never meant to come. He fell to questioning his own motives. There had been smoke in the incense doubtless: there had been blood upon the victim. He was now but thirty years old, with that purity of color and sensitiveness of expression which is said to be nature's reward for a life of spiritual constancy; but he felt that he had parted with youth, and that the "gains for all his losses" could be quickly counted.

It remained for him now only to see Mrs. Eustis and settle on his sister's children an annuity from the money he had kept intact for her use, and to say good-bye to Colonel Harkins. He needed no one to tell him who Colonel Billy Harkins was. It was only as "the Colonel" in a land of gratuitous titles he had failed to recognize him. He would have parted with his right hand if he could so have sundered the connection between them. Did the Colonel perceive how it

galled Bodewin, and privately enjoy his helpless-
ness under the obligation? When the two men
shook hands at parting, Bodewin asked Harkins
to remember that the man who had been as a
brother to his sister should be as a brother to him
in so far as he might be able to serve him or his
in the future.

"All right, brother Bodewin," Harkins replied,
cheerfully, renewing his hard grasp on Bodewin's
hand, and meeting his eyes with a look as hard as
his grasp. "I hope you will know your brother
when you see him again."

All this was now in the past three years. The
mercy Bodewin had been most alive to at the
time was the fact that his mother was no longer
capable of a great sorrow. The stretched chords
had ceased to vibrate. She lived in a painless
dream of the time before the war, when her
husband had been with her and her children had
not left her arms. All that had happened since
then could only be recalled from the outside, and
realized by her with an effort.

CHAPTER X.

THE VALLEY TRAIL.

MRS. CRAIG, having entered upon a scheme
of entertainment for her young guest, pursued it
with enthusiasm. Even the amusements of that
unrestful place and climate took on a certain
fierceness of energy. The mountains were a
perpetual challenge; the valley, with its bright,
sinuous river, running out of sight among gray
willows, a perpetual invitation. Pleasure hurried
its pace at the brief summer's warning. Quick
pulses beat themselves out, and young life that
exulted in perilous effort sank before the prize
was won, and gave place to the next champion of
the hour. Josephine was half fascinated, half
troubled by the spirit of the place. Her morn-
ings were gay, but her evenings were restless and
often mysteriously clouded. With Mrs. Craig as
chaperon and Mr. Hillbury as guide, she had
climbed her peak, had gone down into her mine,

had visited smelting furnaces by night and hydraulic washings by day, had caught her trout in the waters of the "Lake Fork," and had her thrilling gallops in the valley. She had talked and laughed more than ever in her life before, and never had she been, perhaps, less soundly happy. She had met Bodewin constantly, but their acquaintance, which had burst the bud with such a shock, seemed likely to wither half blown. Bodewin had relapsed unexpectedly from his stress of confidence into a silence and backwardness which to Josephine could only signify some decided change in his feelings towards herself. Not to seem to remind him of his former peremptory claim on her sympathy, she carefully avoided any allusion to the day of their long argument on the rocks; nor did Bodewin ever refer to it. They were not often alone together, but when they were, Bodewin found it more difficult than he would have believed to tell his story to this young girl. There was an appalling egotism about it. In one way it would be like telling it to a summer morning. He and his troubles would rest almost as lightly on her consciousness, so he reflected; but the morning did not fix such disturbing eyes upon one's face when appealed to.

One opportunity after another he let slip, until a day came which found him again lounging along in his saddle at Josephine's side. They were riding in the valley with twenty miles of unbroken turf before them, and not a human creature or habitation in sight. Beyond the next long swell there was a milk ranch where they were to wait for Mr. Newbold and Mrs. Craig, but that was yet three miles away. A wind, steady and soft, blowing up through the great gate of the mountains, ruffled the wild grasses on either side the trail. The river showed, in sunny, pebbly reaches, between the pale willows turning silvery in the breeze. The snow-born Arethusa was not swifter-footed or more musical than this unwritten, unsung Arkansas of the high valleys, not a day's journey from its cradle. They had galloped until their blood was up ; they had paced side by side in silence till it had subsided into the warmth that is just enough to give a man daring for a difficult topic of conversation. Bodewin found that he needed all his courage. The summer-morning theory was all very well, but when, at the first grave accent in his voice, Josephine turned upon him that beautiful dark regard he feared and yet longed to meet, his heart grew weak within him. He told his story badly, touching reluctantly on the points where he was sorest, omitting parts of it altogether, and in his dread of overstatement consciously making the worst of his case.

"You understand," he concluded awkwardly, "that when I surveyed Harkins's two claims it was not a business transaction. He did not employ me. I am not a surveyor of mineral claims. Harkins's discovery was one of the first in the camp, and at that time there was not an accredited surveyor within a hundred miles. I offered it as the first service it came in my way to do for him — the first instalment on my debt. You see what a thing it would be to use it against him in court — the record of this affair between us — not of business, but of honor, — to defeat him by means of it. It would be like trapping him in the name of my boasted gratitude. I would rather be shot than do it."

"Still, I think you will do it," Josephine said.

"Would you mind telling me why you think so?"

"Because if you had been satisfied not to do it, those words of mine would have been forgotten as soon as they were spoken."

"I never said I was satisfied *not* to do it, but that is a very different thing from doing it."

Josephine was silent.

"Many things," Bodewin continued, "which are purely matters of private business get abroad in a place like this. Harkins knows I have once positively refused to testify against him. He also knows that I have since been offered in set terms a large sum of money by the parties who wish me to do so."

Josephine blushed painfully at these words, but Bodewin went on without perceiving her embarrassment.

"Stating the situation roughly as a man like Harkins would see it, what motive do you think he would be likely to impute to me were I now to change my mind? Would he not think I had consented to do for money what I had refused to do from an honorable motive?"

"Would he think you had been bribed?" asked Josephine.

Bodewin suddenly remembered that he was on dangerous ground. It was so difficult to keep the fact of Josephine's antecedents in view. He avoided the question.

"Theoretically, of course, Harkins's opinion of

my motives is of no consequence, but actually I cannot afford to disgust him with me while he has this hold upon me. He is capable of anything. Chivalrous as he was to my sister in her extremity, the heart of a gentleman is not in him, or in any of his kind. He would spare no man or woman, living or dead, to reach me, if he believed I had betrayed him. I cannot sacrifice my sister's name even to truth and justice."

"Do the dead require more of us than the living? I am sure no living sister could endure that her brother should be hampered in his public duties by his love for her."

"You have quite the Roman idea of the comparative insignificance of the family claim," said Bodewin, smiling rather bitterly; "but you have a right to it. You come of heroic blood."

Josephine turned upon him. "What do you know of my blood?" she asked, searching his face for the touch of irony she suspected him of. She was restive on the point of blood from a mixture of pride and uneasiness: pride in the strain on her mother's side, and vague distrust of that on her father's, with which she found herself year by year less in sympathy.

Bodewin hastened to repair his blunder. "I beg your pardon. The story of your grandfather's martyrdom has become a part of history, you must remember."

"Yes," said the girl, softening in her quick, responsive way, "the men of my mother's family thought they were truest to their families when they were truest to their own best beliefs. But perhaps you think my grandfather should have yielded everything for the sake of security for his wife and children?"

"Oh, now you are too hard upon me! At the worst, if Harkins were to carry all before him through my poltroonery, it would not be a national crime."

"Oh, wouldn't it? Isn't appropriating other people's goods becoming a national crime? Then we cannot believe our own prophets." Josephine was too young in controversy to have learned to keep the excitement of it out of her voice. She forgot her resolution to abstain from trying to influence Bodewin's decision. She was passionately protesting against it with her eyes and burning cheeks as well as with her words.

"Are you sure it is the family claim after all that is hindering you?" she asked finally. "Is it not your own pride? Are you not trying to cancel a private debt by neglecting a public duty?"

Bodewin's answer came slowly. He had asked himself a hundred times why he should sacrifice to the protection of another man's property that which was much dearer to him than any tangible possessions of his own. But between these two the question had never been for one moment a question of property; each would have scorned in the other the first intimation that it could be. Bodewin only said, "What impossible beings you must think us! If you knew men better, you would not expect so much of us."

"Do you call it so much? I shall never expect less — never — of any man I believe in!"

The ranch was now in sight, and they rode the rest of the way in silence. Not one of the family, except the cows, was at home, nor were Mrs. Craig and Mr. Newbold anywhere to be seen. A paper pinned on the door bore an explanation in Mrs. Craig's handwriting.

"Ranchman's wife at the railroad camp. We are going on there to see her about the eggs. Wait for us or not, as you please."

The railroad camp was a mile distant up the valley. They decided to wait. Bodewin dismounted, and lifted Josephine from her saddle. She found a seat on a long bench against the side wall of the larger cabin; while Bodewin looked about the premises to make sure no one was at home. Two long, low cabins, of unhewn logs, built about four feet apart, were united by their roofs. The covered way between framed a view of the valley in the slanting light of afternoon. Through the uncurtained windows it could be seen that one of the cabins was used for a dwelling and the other for granary, barn, stable, wood-shed, and other purposes. Its interior was crammed like a schoolboy's pocket, and was nearly as dark. Absolutely, the place was deserted, except by the cows, pensively chewing their cuds in the corral behind the cabin.

Bodewin seated himself on the bench near Josephine. He took off his soft felt hat, and crushed it on the angle of his knee. As he leaned forward on his elbows, his profile strongly illumined in the sun's level light, certain merits in his appearance which had escaped Josephine's diffident observation now struck her for the first time. His eyes, that she had thought were black, proved to be a dark hazel-gray. The wind loosened a lock of his close-cut hair, brushed with unbecoming severity of outline, and blew it across his forehead. Instantly he looked the younger and the better for it. She noted the modelling of his bent head, the delicacy of his complexion where his hat had shaded it from the sun, the high, clear-cut lines of his face. He looked like some keen-edged instrument, fit for precise and subtle uses. He had not found his true work as yet, that was evident; and Josephine vaguely wondered whether so efficient an instrument carelessly handled might not be dangerous to others, or itself get dulled or broken.

While they waited, the sun's red disk touched the mountains; it dropped out of sight; the mountains darkened against the after-glow that spread broadly over the plain and flamed upward, gilding the long cloud-islands that rested in the upper region of the sky.

"Mr. Bodewin," said Josephine, after one of those silences that often fell between these two unconventional acquaintances, "why should you feel that you alone are responsible for your sister's marriage? She had a mother as well as a brother; and you were very young."

"My mother was scarcely in the world that summer. She lived with her dead. And she was broken — by — "

"Forgive me!" Josephine interrupted.

"You do not hurt me. Say anything to me you like. It helps me."

"I would like to say one thing more, if I may. I am sure it would trouble your sister's rest if she could hear you saying what you did just now — that she had a mortgage on your life for all, you were worth, and that now a part of it had fallen into base hands. Can any one hold a mortgage on our lives except the Giver of life itself? It seems to me you leave out — God."

"Would you have me throw the consequences of my carelessness upon Him?"

"I would have you believe that your sister was in His care as well as in yours."

"It would make a pagan of me if I could believe God meant her life to be what we made it, among us."

"I am afraid you are a pagan already."

"Very likely. And being a pagan, I am also a coward."

Josephine hated to hear a man call himself a coward, even for the sake of being contradicted. She hesitated, and then, smiling, said deliberately, as if speaking by rote, —

"'I would not hear thine enemy say so.'"

Bodewin smiled too, rather sadly.

"The context made you say that; but you do not mean it."

"I can never tell how much I mean until I am tried," she said, "but I think I mean it."

"What should you say to one who called me a coward?"

"I should say that if you were it could only be as 'conscience doth make cowards of us all.' And to myself I should add — morbid conscience."

"You think I am morbid?"

"I hope you are; for if your views of our mutual accountability are true, then life is not difficult — it is impossible."

"Well, is it not impossible? Life, as it was meant to be?"

"I do not know how it was meant to be. I believe that it is, that it will be, full of happiness — I do not mean pleasure — to those who hunger and thirst after righteousness, even if they make terrible, terrible mistakes. I cannot believe in those fatalities which make one man the destroyer of another, whether he wills it or not. The intention must count for something."

"We cannot live by our intentions," said Bodewin. "I think I see your father and Mrs. Craig coming. They are a long way off; do you see? Where the trail cuts in towards Bird's Eye Cañon."

"I wish they had come before I began to talk of things that are beyond me," sighed Josephine.

"There is nothing beyond you — nothing worth mentioning."

Whenever Bodewin said anything to Josephine that she might have resented as flattering in its tendency, he did it with a dismal reluctance which made it a thing to pity him for.

He was getting restive under a deepening sense of her truth and sweetness. He would have been glad to find a flaw in her — another flaw; for since he had made her atone to the uttermost for that slip with which their acquaintance had begun, she had been steadily triumphing in his thoughts.

He had long ceased to be even amused at their relations to each other with reference to the trial — Mr. Newbold's daughter helping her father to his most important witness. He would have felt like choking any man who dared to hint at the convenience of such an arrangement for Mr. Newbold. He adored her unconscious sincerity that ignored the world and feared no misconception; and he felt the tribute to his own manhood it so simply

yet subtly conveyed. He was able to speak of
her to Hillbury that evening with calmness, however, and to agree with his friend in his favorite
theory, that a woman must have a certain amount
of self-consciousness to escape being crude. Hillbury was apt to take a cool, disparaging tone in
speaking of the average pretty woman, but Bodewin could not believe in Hillbury's entire indifference to a girl he himself found so charming.

CHAPTER XI.

AN ANONYMOUS LETTER.

BODEWIN had left his horse at the stable, and had overtaken Hillbury as the latter was strolling along the ditch-walk, reading his letters on his way back to camp. Hillbury put up the letters as Bodewin fell into step beside him.

"I tried to find you this afternoon, Bodewin. Where are your rooms now?"

"Rooms! My *room* is in the Parker building, second story, front, if you want to see me on business."

"You have more than one room there."

"Well, if you count a man's bedroom."

"I wanted to tell you you've won your cigars."

"What cigars?"

"Have you forgotten our bet about Craig's cabin?"

"Craig's cabin?"

"The cabin in the Lake woods; the girl-and-pup story."

Bodewin's face changed slightly as he replied, " Yes, I remember."

The mention of the Lake woods called up other impressions more vivid than those connected with Craig's adventure.

" You were right about Craig ; there is no cabin there."

" What did I say about Craig ? "

" You said the little boy lied; and apparently he did."

After a pause Bodewin said, " Craig may have lied on occasion, but he is not a liar. If I ever said that he was, or implied it, I lied myself."

" Well, the cabin cannot be found. I'll send the cigars around to-morrow."

" I won't take them ; do you understand? I don't want to smoke a whole box of cigars flavored with a stupid fiction of Craig's.   I'd rather borrow them of you one at a time," he added, as Hillbury looked grave, " and no thanks to Craig."

" You still insist there is no cabin ? " Hillbury persisted.

" Hang the cabin ! "

His words, few as they had been, convinced Hillbury that Bodewin was himself surprised that the cabin could not be found. His pretended incredulity, he believed, must have been pure recklessness, founded on his dislike to everything Craig did, or the joking of a tired and hungry man; or else, for some reason impossible to guess, Bodewin had not been perfectly frank. The impression was so strong that Hillbury resolved to make one more search for evidence of the truth of Craig's story.

The outer door of Bodewin's office in the Parker building had a slit in it, and a box nailed on the inner panel for the convenience of callers in his absence. When he returned to his lodgings that evening, Bodewin, after striking a light, examined this box. It contained but one letter, from a most unattractive correspondent, to judge by the superscription. The envelope bore no postmark; the letter was undated. It read as follows:—

"Do not go on the witness stand unprotected. Colonel Harkins swears that if you testify against him you shall not leave the court-room alive. A Friend."

Bodewin sent a letter to Craig that night, short but carefully worded.

His testimony, he wrote, in the case between the Eagle Bird and Uinta mines was at the service of the Eagle Bird. He would prefer to give it in response to a subpoena in due form. He would take his expenses and the usual witness-fee, nothing more, and the question of money need not be referred to again in regard to this case; and he was Mr. Craig's respectfully. This letter Mr. Craig handed to Mr. Newbold the next day as they sat together on the Eagle Bird piazza, waiting to see the superintendent on a small matter connected with the lawsuit,—a matter which made it necessary for Sammis to look up some old maps of the mine. Josephine had gone into the house to see Mrs. Sammis's baby. She had found him in the dining-room, seated in his high-chair at a table where his mother was engaged in cutting out the overskirt of a new grenadine dress. Josephine was consulted as to the proper length to allow for draping, and as baby gave more of his assistance than was desirable, making dashes at the paper patterns, and side pulls at the stuff spread smoothly on the table, Josephine seized him out of his chair and bore him off into the front room, where she made him happy in a way he knew well. She placed him on her knee, facing her, at arm's length, and, with her smiling eyes fixed on his solemn ones, began softly jogging him up and down to the recitative, "This is the way the lady rides," etc. As the pace grew

better, his fat shoulders began to shake and the
dimples to show round the deep-sunk corners of
his mouth; but when it came to "Hobble-de-gee
the farmer goes!" his content knew no bounds.
Now they began once more with "This is the way
the lady rides, nimble namble, nimble namble,"
and the gait was so easy and the song so low to
match it, that Josephine could hear her father's
voice speaking to Mr. Craig in the porch outside.
The shutters were drawn together, but the windows were open.

"Well, what did I tell you? It has come out
just as I said it would!"

"How was that, Mr. Newbold?"

"Don't you remember what I said to you down
there in your office?"

"About Bodewin? You said, if I'm not mistaken, that his case called for a woman's influence; wasn't that it?"

"Well, what I meant was the social thing, you
know. Of course, you can't have society without
women. He has seen a good deal of us lately,
and naturally he takes more interest in the case.
He's reconsidered the matter from a more human
point of view."

"He has not seen much of me lately. He has

seen a good deal of my wife and of your daughter. Is that the point of view you call human?"

"You lawyers are the worst fellows to turn a man's words wrong side out. You know very well what I mean. Bodewin has come round — most unexpectedly to you, but not to me. I knew he was coming. The rides and the talks and the little dinners have done the business, and now you can come in with the majesty of the law and claim the credit of it."

"To whom is the credit due, do you think — your daughter or my wife?"

"Oh, come, Craig! I'm not going to quarrel with you — not until after the trial."

"There will not be any trial with me for your counsel, Mr. Newbold, unless you drop that little theory of yours, pretty sudden too! You can give all the credit you like to your daughter, — I beg her pardon, and you ought to too, — but I want you to understand, before we go any further, that my wife doesn't help me to win my cases."

"Good Lord, man! one would suppose—" Josephine sprang up, hardly conscious of the heavy child in her arms, and carried him back to the dining-room, where Mrs. Sammis was folding up the breadths of her overskirt.

"I do believe there is enough left for a shoulder-cape," she said, without looking up, as Josephine entered. "Don't you like those little shirred capes?"

"On some people — yes," Josephine replied, absently.

"If there wasn't enough to shir, I might put some fringe around it, and trim it with passymentery. — Ain't you been tiring yourself out with him? You look real warm!" She held out her hands for the child.

"He doesn't tire me — does he, monkins?" Josephine leaned her head against the baby's clean white pinafore, put on over yesterday's frock with especial reference to her visit. He clasped the bent, dark head in his chubby arms, patted it vigorously, and then pushed himself away from her that he might peep down into her face. Mrs. Sammis looked on with flattered regard.

"You've got a real way with babies!" she said. "For an only child yourself it's wonderful. I guess you're one of the born mothers. You must look out when it comes to marrying. When you see a girl with blood in her for two, she's sure to pick out a man that hasn't half enough for one, and nurse him the rest of her life, and be as proud of him, like as not, as if he was her first-born, and think he's got a terrible intellect."

Josephine, in her visits to the mine, had been in the habit of using the Sammis baby as an innocent sort of buffer to ward off the mother's attentions. That day she kept the child in her arms, petting him and recklessly encouraging his small tyrannies, until the horses were brought round and her father called to her from the piazza that it was time to go.

Nothing in all her life had ever hurt her like those words of his she had overheard. Josephine had ever been too ready to flame out on slight provocation, and dispute the paternal judgment and sometimes the paternal authority on trifling points, but this issue involved differences too vital even for discussion. She could not open the subject to her father without showing him her scorn for his point of view. All the satisfaction she might have had in Bodewin's conversion was blighted. Reviewing his several conversations with her as she was able to recall them, she fancied she could read her own humiliation in his cold surprise, his mocking appeal, his abrupt and intimate demand. The first slip had been hers, but she was now ready to believe her father had done his best to put her in the way of making it. He who should have saved her from her faults had been in league with them against her — was openly exulting in their consequences, with an indecency of suggestion which had disgusted even Mr. Craig. The object of her soliloquy was meanwhile comfortably riding behind her, by the side of Mr. Craig, talking of future improvements at the mine, to be begun as soon as the trial was over. For now that Bodewin had been won, Mr. Newbold, and his lawyer no less, regarded the case as virtually decided in their favor.

CHAPTER XII.

DEAD OR MISSING.

MR. NEWBOLD wondered a little that Josephine's interest in the trial should have so suddenly cooled. But no doubt she was tired of the subject; it had been presented to her somewhat monotonously of late. She declined to go down with him to Denver on the week of the trial, preferring to stay at the mine with Mrs. Sammis. It would not be an exciting visit, but Josephine would have chosen to go back alone to Kansas City rather than make one of the Eagle Bird party on this conspicuous occasion. Mr. Newbold had hired a light mountain-wagon and a team of horses to carry his constituents over the range to the end of the track in the safest and speediest manner. He had also ordered the best breakfast the Wiltsie House could furnish, to be served at the mine, where the party were to meet on the morning of the journey.

156

Bodewin had been as good as his word when he told Josephine that he would take no advantage of her reluctant consideration of his difficulty. She had not seconded her father's numerous invitations to him, and had met him only through their mutual acquaintances, Mrs. Craig and Hillbury. One of Mrs. Craig's children had been ill, and the outdoor gayeties of her planning had ceased for a week before the date of the trial. During this time Josephine had not seen Bodewin. She would gladly have escaped the breakfast, but her father had made a point of her presiding. However, to her great relief, Bodewin was not among the guests. At the last moment he had resigned his seat in the wagon and announced that he would make the pass on horseback.

"We shall see you to-morrow at breakfast?" Mr. Newbold had asked, and Bodewin had begged to be excused, as he was not an early breakfaster and would not need to start as soon as the team, by an hour at least. He came loitering up the trail a few minutes after the Eagle Bird party had set off. He had left his waterproof coat in Sammis's office the last time he had gone through the mine, he said, and had stopped for it on his way.

Josephine was sitting on the steps of the high porch as he rode up. He had seen her, and it was too late for her to escape into the house. She smiled collectedly enough and said good-morning, while Mrs. Sammis came from the end of the porch, holding a leaky watering-pot at arm's length, to ask if he would not change his mind and have some breakfast. He had had a cup of coffee before leaving the camp, he thanked her, but would she kindly send some one for that coat? The office was locked and Sammis had taken the key, but Mrs. Sammis thought she knew where there was another key that would fit. She went into the house to find it, and Bodewin seated himself on the steps below Josephine. His first look at her, before a word had been spoken, assured Josephine that she was safe at least in his regard. But that did not take away her trouble by any means. It might have been better that he should despise her. No one could have guessed from Josephine's appearance that she was unhappy, still less humiliated, about any-thing. Bodewin was looking at her timidly; he had never seen her before in a white dress. It was only a white flannel, made in the simplest way, but a garment of white samite could not have been more mystic and wonderful to Bodewin's inexperienced eyes. It defined her fair arms and shoulders and clung in some mysterious way about her hips, sweeping downward in long soft folds over the pleatings that huddled about her feet. Bodewin could not venture to more than glance at her as she sat on the steps above him. It was scarcely possible to avoid some reference to the object of his journey.

"Are you surprised at my going, after all I said to you that last time?" he asked.

"No; I knew then, in spite of what you said, that you would go."

"Thank you for your faith in me. I ought to be uncommonly happy, I suppose. True happiness consists in doing what is disagreeable, doesn't it?"

Now that Bodewin had begun to talk in this safe, artificial strain, Josephine's courage returned.

"Perhaps so," she said, "if you do it for the sake of something better than happiness."

"You are the most exacting young moralist! Isn't it enough that you have got me on the right track at last, without asking for my passport?"

Josephine's face turned scarlet.

"I have had nothing to do with the track that you are on."

"Am I not your witness?"

"You know that you are not. Remember, the condition of my listening to you was that you should not make it personal."

"You repudiate me altogether now that I am doing what you wished me to do. You don't deny that you do wish it?"

"If it is merely a question of what I or any one else wishes you to do, you had better not do it."

Poor Josephine was insisting all the more strenuously on the dignity of her position, now that she herself had lost all faith in it; and Bodewin was irritated by this display of rectitude, when he was longing for something less comfortless to a man starting on a journey attended by risks known to no one but himself.

"Such very abstract views of duty as yours strike me as a little inhuman," he said, — "to adore a man's duty and yet spurn him for doing it."

"I do not spurn you; neither do I intend to applaud you."

"I don't ask you to; I ask only a kind word of

good-bye, and some little recognition of the fact that I am going on your errand. That is very weak of me, perhaps."

"But you are not going on my errand. What right have I to send you on my errands, or you to go?"

"I might go on your errand without your sending me."

Josephine shook her head. "How can you play with a serious decision like this, even for the sake of teasing?"

"Why should it tease you? I should be glad to relieve you from that horror you seem to have of any complicity in my acts; but I hardly think I should be riding over the range to-day if you had not challenged my right to do as I pleased."

Since there was no denying that his motives were mixed, Bodewin was resolved to get what comfort he could out of the mixture. He wished Josephine to feel that this act of his was in some sort a bond between them, and she resisted the acknowledgment he was forcing upon her, with maidenly fierceness.

She stood up, facing him, obliging him to rise, though he was in no hurry to go. He leaned heavily on the balustrade, avoiding her eyes.

"Don't go," she said, more gently; "don't give your testimony from any motive lower than the one which made you withhold it."

"Be satisfied," he said; "I am doing what is right. I don't ask myself why I am doing it," — he lifted his heavy-lidded, passionate eyes to her face, — "and you must not ask me, because I might tell you the truth."

He took off his hat and silently offered his hand. Josephine let him hold hers a moment, and they parted without looking at each other again. As Bodewin was unhitching his horse Mrs. Sammis appeared.

"You're not going without your coat, Mr. Bodewin?" She came down the steps with it, apologizing for having kept him waiting so long. "I hope you won't have to ride too fast to make up the time."

Bodewin assured her he had plenty of time. He rolled up the coat into a snug bundle and tied it securely with the leathern thongs attached to the back of his saddle, swung himself on his horse, and, lifting his hat to Mrs. Sammis, rode away.

Twilight drew the curtains of sunset in the valley. Night came on, and the Eagle Bird

folded its murky wings in such rest as its cease-
less subterranean life permitted. Josephine sat
on the porch steps. She had been alone nearly
all day, for, though nominally the guest of the
superintendent's wife, she saw very little of her
hostess. The superintendent had married, as in
small, isolated communities, the average man mar-
ries, the woman he had seen most frequently. In
Sammis's case she had happened to be a garrulous
soul in an under-vitalized body. Mrs. Sammis
had stamped her feebleness with the force of a
fatality on her husband's life, his house, and his
children, suffering herself more than Sammis, perhaps, from this repetition of her own negative
personality. There was a dreary inefficiency
about the conduct of affairs in the household she
now found herself part of, that had already begun
to weigh upon Josephine like a trouble of her
own.

At the dump station below the hill a light had
shone since twilight. At intervals she heard the
hollow rolling of a car along the tramway. As
the sound ceased, a bolt rattled, and the torrent
of earth and stones crashed over the dump. The
car rolled back into the tunnel, and in the suc-
ceeding silence the strokes of the engine from the

shaft-house counted the hours to the change of shifts. Presently a new sound caught Josephine's attention — the light, sharp click of a horse's hoofs coming rapidly up the hill. She lost it for an instant, then she heard it again, nearing faster and now close at hand. By the main group of buildings it stopped, and voices of men were heard talking.

Mrs. Sammis came out on the porch, carrying the baby, her apron turned up over its bare head. She walked past Josephine to the end of the porch, and called into the darkness: —

"Whose horse is that?"

There was no audible reply, and she repeated the question. "Whose *horse* is that?"

"Is anything the matter?" Josephine asked. She too went to the end of the porch, and looked and listened with Mrs. Sammis in the contagion of vague alarm.

"I thought that horse coming up just now was the bald-faced one Mr. Bodewin rode," Mrs. Sammis said.

"Has Mr. Bodewin come *back?*"

"It wasn't Bodewin rode him in. I saw him plain enough coming up the hill. It was that man from Lounsberry stables. I can't ever think of his name. He brings your father's horses."

"But where is Mr. Bodewin?"

"That's what I'd like to know, if I could get anything out of them men!"

"Let me take the baby, Mrs. Sammis."

The sleepy child began to scream when his mother transferred him to Josephine's arms. She carried him into the house, and walked up and down the close entry with him, mechanically hushing his cries, while Mrs. Sammis ran out to the stable to make inquiries.

"Oh, baby, baby, *do* hush!" Josephine almost sobbed herself, trying to listen.

In a few moments Mrs. Sammis returned. The baby was still screaming; and with a mother's sententious sympathy she took her offspring into her own arms and carried him into her bedroom, where Josephine heard her singing her habitual lullaby —

> "Safe in the arms of Jesus,
> Safe on His gentle breast."

The measured creak of a rocking-chair continued for some time after the singing had ceased. Then Mrs. Sammis came out of the room, carrying a smoky kerosene lamp in her hand. She placed it in the centre of a table with a red printed cotton cover on it, re-arranged the books in little set piles around the lamp, and finally sat down by Josephine at the window, sighing audibly and stroking back her hair with her thin, moist, bleached-looking hands.

"Well," she said, "*they* don't know what's gone of him any more'n we do! That bay horse of his come in alone about seven o'clock, and walked himself into the stable where he's kep', and that's all they know. They waited till the stage got in; but there wasn't any message from our folks. They passed our team the other side of the summit; but they hadn't seen any sign of him either side. He hadn't stopped at English George's, but just at the foot of the pass,—you rec'lect, when you come in, that little gulch where the water was, and right smart of grass? The woman says she was just takin' some blackberry pies out of the oven,—one of them outdoor ovens, you've seen 'em,—and he rode up and bought one of the pies, and et it settin' on his horse, and took a big drink of milk, and gave her a dollar. 'Twasn't more'n three bits' worth. They sent up from the stable to know if he changed his horse here this morning before he started. *You* saw him tie that coat on to his saddle, didn't you?"

" Yes," said Josephine.

" Well, *they* say the saddle came home bare."

" Bare ? "

" There wasn't any coat or nothing tied fast to it."

" What does that mean ? "

" It means it wasn't an accident." Mrs. Sammis lowered her voice to give greater effect to her next words. " They think, down to the camp, it's some of the Uinta's work. The horse had been hit by a bullet, and they say the mark of it showed it come from behind. There is no tellin'," she continued, after a pause, which brought no comment from Josephine. " Some thinks he's just been playin' into their hands all along. He give 'em a first-rate chance, goin' off alone like that. Sammis has 'lowed all along that he was in with them."

Josephine rose, and went out on the porch. The air was of an unusual softness. The stars between the pine trunks seemed few and very far away. She watched the light of a lantern swinging from the hand of the night foreman, who was crossing the trodden space before the shaft-house, and listened to the sluff, sluff, of his rubber boots, as their loose tops rubbed together at every step. The light at the dump station was eclipsed, and now again came the rattling of the bolt and the plunging of the load over the dump. It fell into the echoless silence of the wood like a stone in a deep well. So had the news of the night fallen into Josephine's heart. She heard Mrs. Sammis's step in the hall, and turned to say: —

"Will you tell me as soon as you know anything more, — whatever it is? I want to know it."

"Why, of course; why shouldn't you know it?"

Why, indeed, Josephine repeated to herself, should she be spared the knowledge of Bodewin's fate? What was it to her but one more man added to the list of the camp's missing, or dead, or dishonored?

CHAPTER XIII.

ON THE ROAD TO THE PASS.

It was nearly noon when Bodewin reached the foot of the pass. He had left the ticklish places on his road behind him — the deep woods, the wet stony hollows, the winding gulches with high rocky walls that shut out the sun. The secluded trail he had taken now met the stage road, where passengers were frequent. The chances for an adventure on that exposed highway were hardly worth considering. Bodewin kept a quietly watchful eye on each turn of the road or projecting angle of rock, as a matter of habit, rather than of special precaution.

As he slowly climbed the last half mile to the summit, he heard some one shouting, and, looking back, saw a man on a hard-ridden horse motioning to him from a distance. He waited for the stranger to overtake him.

"If your name is Bodewin, there's a man back here in the timber has got some papers for you."

Bodewin looked hard at his fellow-traveller. He was a man of about fifty, with a tall, stooping figure, a foxy beard that was turning gray, and a scar on the side of his thin nose that made his eyes seem closer together.

"All right, boss!" he said. "Take a good look at me. It sounds like a lie, but it ain't."

"Where does your man say he's from?" Bodewin asked.

"He came out from camp, just behind you. Says he is one of the men from Lounsberry's stables. Some papers belongin' to a party named Newbold got left at the Eagle Bird mine. The women folks found 'em just after you'd gone. The young lady there, Newbold's daughter, knew they'd be wanted on the trial that's coming off to-morrow, and she chartered him to overtake you with 'em. He promised her he wouldn't give 'em into no hands only yourn."

"Well," said Bodewin, "what is he doing in the timber?"

"Horse fell on him. He's all broke up. I come along just after he was hurt, and he got me to overtake you and git you to come back for the papers. I told him you wouldn't come, and to give me the papers. I might be all right, he said, but he couldn't let 'em out of his hands."

The ingenuousness of this speech was not borne out by the speaker's countenance, but various considerations were working on Bodewin during the few seconds it took him to choose between the risks of believing a false story and doubting a true one.

"Are you goin' back?" the man inquired. "*I'm* goin'. I want to git him into shape, so's he can git back to camp."

"Hold on a minute. Where did you say this man was?"

"Back here half a mile in the timber."

"All right," Bodewin said. "Go on. I'm with you."

The stranger did not look back or wait for Bodewin, but turned his horse's head down the hill again. He turned off from the stage road into the trail by which Bodewin had come. They were soon among the trees — the stunted pines and spruces, straggling ahead of the close columns of the main forest. Here Bodewin met with evidence confirmatory of his friend's story. A gray horse could plainly be seen a short distance ahead of them, foraging for a bite by the wayside, while near him in the sparse shade lay a man at full length on the ground. Bodewin thought he could remember having seen such a light-gray horse with white mane and tail at Lounsberry's stables. He was sure he remembered the man's face, when he came near enough to see it. He was that dark, dull-eyed youth, partner of the Irishman whom Bodewin had conversed with at his claim on the mountain. Bodewin was not surprised to find the prospector, two weeks later, a stableman. It was the way of the camp.

"You don't remember me, Mr. Bodewin," the young fellow said, lifting his sullen black eyes to Bodewin's face. "But I know you." He opened his coat and took hold of some papers that showed, projecting from an inside pocket.

"Here's the papers she told me to give you; I can't raise up." His face was darkly flushed, as with pain.

"You don't need to get off, Mr. Bodewin," the other man said. "I can hand 'em to you."

"No, you can't," the messenger objected. "I promised her I'd give 'em into his hands or fetch 'em back to her; and I won't lie to her to save him gettin' off his horse. G——! how my leg hurts!"

With his first unguarded impulse Bodewin dropped from his saddle to the ground, and stooped frankly and compassionately to receive the papers; and at the instant he stooped he felt his pistol leaving his pistol-pocket. A hand had withdrawn it from behind. It was the hand of his ingenuous guide. Turning sharply as he straightened himself, Bodewin's head nearly touched the muzzle of another revolver.

"Stop!" a hard voice called. "If you move you're a dead man."

Bodewin did not move. A second reason for not moving had presented itself in the shape of a pistol held against the other side of his head by Miss Newbold's faithful messenger. One deep and fervent curse escaped him, and then Bodewin asked, — "What do you want?"

"We want *you*," the man with the scar replied. "Will you come along with us, or do you want to fight?"

"Fight!" said Bodewin. "I've got a good show, haven't I?"

"We're a little too soon for you, that's a fact. Tie his hands, Tony."

"You needn't tie my hands," Bodewin expostulated. "I will go along all right."

"You'd better mean it, if you say so. We don't want to have to hurt you."

"I don't intend to get hurt. What are you going to do with me?"

"We're goin' to keep you kind of quiet for a few days. You won't have a bad time of it, if you're peaceable. We'll have to cover your eyes, Mr. Bodewin. We don't want you to get too intimate with the road we're goin'. Hand me the rag, Tony."

"Would you mind taking my handkerchief?" Bodewin asked.

The man with the scar considerately made use of Bodewin's handkerchief to bind his eyes, instead of a degraded piece of calico which looked like part of a woman's apron.

"This horse will not lead," Bodewin said when the party was mounted and ready to move; "but he will follow all right if I tell him to. One of you can ride ahead and the other behind me. I will promise not to make a break between here and your camp."

"I'll take your word on that, boss." The elder man had dropped his hard business tone for the semi-confidential drawl he reserved for social purposes. "Tony, you can lead off, and I'll close up the percession."

"And you'll do the talkin'," Tony remarked.

"Well, if I don't talk I can't say nothin'," the elder man retorted.

The procession moved on in single file, Bodewin, disarmed and blindfolded, between his two captors. He had not been in a moment's doubt as to the author of this wayside pleasantry. The plan of his capture, he was convinced, had originated in a subtler brain than either of those selected to carry it out. What chiefly hurt him was the thought that his disappearance might be misunderstood by his friends of the Eagle Bird. His promise to appear at the trial had delayed the serving of the subpœna; they might conclude, if disposed to doubt his good faith, that he had availed himself of this solitary ride to give them the slip, even were it not planned for that purpose. If he could but send some message back! The thing seemed as little possible as to escape himself. All that, however, could wait. Deprived of eyesight, his remaining senses were doubly on the alert to report each feature of the road. By the sound of his horse's feet he knew they were still on the trail. They followed it but a short distance, perhaps from fear of meeting other passengers, then, turning to the left, struck

across a gravelly ridge. Bodewin recognized it as
one of those numerous lateral moraines making
lesser valleys at right angles to the great valley
of the Arkansas. The plan of march was not
adapted to conversation. Occasionally a voice
would admonish Bodewin: —

" Down your head there, pardner ! Dodge that
tree limb"; "Watch out for them quaking asps";
or " Mind that badger-hole on the up-hill side."

The ridge, inclining always toward the valley,
dipped suddenly, and the horses took the slide one
after another, carrying soil and stones with them.
Bodewin made no attempt to guide his horse. He
had trusted Baldy's feet and Baldy's eyes on
many a dark night and blind trail. At the foot
of the ridge they crossed a piece of timber, and
beyond it Bodewin could hear the horses' hoofs
sucking through the swampy bottom. Now they
were rustling past a willow thicket, now wading
into the coarse, bunchy grass of the valley pastur-
age; southward again, the soft valley wind in
their faces, the sun declining from the zenith
towards the west. Now into a gorge, grassy at
first and wet, then steep and stony, with a coolness as of rocks high and near. Bodewin was
positive they had not crossed the valley. The

plan was probably to wind him in and out between those narrow divides which radiate from each great peak downwards into the valley, until he had become · confused, then double on their track and bring him to some spot not far from the camp itself. Another reason for making such a mystery of their route occurred to Bodewin. His abductors no doubt were arranging matters so that after his release he should not be able to swear to the place where he had been detained.

The last hour of the ride was through uninterrupted woods, and here no idea of their direction could be had. They were not the burnt woods; the shade was close and dark, the horses' feet sounded hollow on the muffled ground.

"In sight of camp, pardner," said the elder guide. "You can pull off the blinders."

Bodewin took the handkerchief from his eyes and looked about him with keen interest. He was turning a new page of his experience, which was likely to prove exciting, if not instructive. The wood was in shadow. Only in the tree-tops the sunlight lingered, letting fall a gleam here and there, to burnish a trunk, or speckle with tawny lights the dark-red forest floor. Beautiful and solemn and peaceful as night itself, the pine

woods stretched before him. Was not this a
better ending to a day's journey than the one he
had set out for? — the crowd on the platform at
the new railroad terminus, the noisy carload of
people, the train banging along the break-neck
grades of the Platte Cañon, and the trial and the
witness-stand? The decision had been taken out
of his hands, and Harkins was getting even with
his debtor in a unique fashion of his own. Bodewin's courage was of a deliberate and philosophic
kind. He was too indifferent to danger to
seek it, nor was he possessed by that necessity to
fight under any provocation which belongs to men
of the "game" variety. He was game in a somewhat different sense. He had remained quiet
when he found himself disarmed, with a pistol at
each ear, not from fear of the pistols, but from an
objection to an illogical suicide. His blood had
been cool enough to let his mind work, and to
Bodewin's mind to have invited death at such
hands, and in such a manner, would have been
supremely objectless and silly. Yet there was a
taint of moral poltroonery in him. It revealed
itself in the relief with which he welcomed the
utter irresponsibility of his situation. From a
man who had been morbidly conscious of his

responsibilities, he had become one who was sick of the very word. He was almost glad to be deprived of his rights for a time, that he might enjoy a corresponding suspension of his duties. He had got down now to the ground floor of social ethics, where the law of self-preservation was uncomplicated by subtleties of mutual obligation.

"In sight of camp," the man with the scar had announced — and now the camp itself was close at hand. Where had he known this place before? The long-backed cabin, overtopped by the dump of a deserted prospect-hole, the bench under the projecting roof, the little corral. This was Craig's cabin, beyond a doubt, even though Hillbury had failed to find it. Bodewin was charmed by the sequence of events.

CHAPTER XIV.

THE three men dismounted at the door of the cabin, leaving their horses standing. Bodewin untied his blanket roll and rubber coat from the back of his saddle, and tossed them on the bench beside the door, while Tony, seated on the bench, kept an eye upon him. The elder man, whom Tony called Dad, had gone into the cabin. In a few minutes he returned, laughing and shaking his head.

Tony's look expressed sulky inquiry as to the cause of his merriment.

" Babe's mad," he explained. "Says she won't have no men folks round, inside there, till grub's ready."

" What's she mad about now ? " asked Tony.

" About this yer company we brought home," said Dad, winking at Bodewin. "She 'lows she don't take no hand in this kind of entertainment. She'll give you enough to eat, though," he added.

"Why don't you go in there and make her quit?" Tony suggested.

"Go in yourself, if you want to. I've learned to let women folks alone when they are plumb full o' mad."

Tony went to the door and tried to open it. It was fastened from within.

"Babe!" he called, " *Oh*, Babe! Come out yer! *Ain't* ye 'shamed!—Give you a dollar if she don't come," he said to Bodewin parenthetically.

Bodewin laughed.

"Give you forty if she does!" Dad jeered.

Tony continued calling and pounding until the door on a sudden was violently thrown back and Babe herself appeared on the threshold, fronting the cool daylight, with a glow of firelight behind her, which reddened the murky interior of the cabin.

Babe was a tall, white-throated, full-bosomed girl of seventeen, at this moment red with wrath, her blue eyes big and dark under her low, flat, white brow. Her skin was white as birch-wood stripped of its bark, but under it were muscles as tough as Tony's own.

"Who's callin' Babe round yer?"

The words were flung out with a look intended

for Tony. But Tony had retired as the door opened, and the look fell hot from the stormy blue eyes into Bodewin's cool gray ones, as he leaned a little forward from his seat on the bench. One look was enough. Babe retreated, banging the door behind her. Dad and Tony burst into loud laughter, Dad fairly shedding tears in his excess of mirth.

"Babe wilted then, for sure!" said Tony; and Dad, turning to Bodewin, who had remained perfectly grave, apologized for his daughter.

"Babe's always skeered of strangers; she don't mean nothin'. Here you, Tony, quit laughin' at your sister, and go take care of them critters!"

The two horses which were at home had strayed off towards the corral, while Baldy, observant of his master's movements, remained near the cabin. Tony walked leisurely towards him, and put out his hand to take his bridle-rein. Baldy jumped away a few feet. Tony stepped quickly after him and caught at the rein. Baldy whirled off and let fly at Tony with his heels. Bodewin smiled, and Dad looked interested.

"Stop your jumpin' and go to him quietlike and speak to him," he suggested.

Tony replied with a scornful jerk of his head,

and made another rush for Baldy's rein, calling, "Whoa, there!" Baldy swerved, reared, tossing his rein up in the air out of Tony's reach.

"That's right, Tony, cuss a little; maybe that'll git him." Dad chuckled and Bodewin laughed outright.

"He can't catch that horse; he won't let any one catch him but me."

Tony heard Bodewin's remark.

"I'll bet, by ——, I can catch him!" he said.

Returning to the cabin, he took down a coiled lasso that hung within convenient reach by the door.

Dad and Bodewin watched him in silence as he adjusted the rope for a throw. Baldy had trotted off a little way. As Tony ran towards him swinging the rope above his head, the horse stopped and seemed to wait for the throw. The rope left Tony's hand, the loop widened, and Baldy, standing perfectly still, put his long white nose to the sod. The lasso settled down upon his neck and shoulders, and slid harmless to the ground. Baldy gave one quick jump sideways, then walked away, turning his sagacious eye backward towards his master.

"Lawd in the mornin'!" Dad exclaimed, smiting

his knees with both hands, "but that horse has got sense! How'd you l'arn him not to leave no handle for the lass' to ketch on?"

Tony made another run for the horse and another throw, but again Baldy was as a graven image, with his nose and all four feet touching the ground.

Bodewin now stood up and called him to him. Baldy came at the word and stood beside his master, with an imperturbable gravity and innocence in his white-eyelashed eyes. Bodewin waited, stroking Baldy's nose, until Tony, panting and swearing, had drawn near. Then he said, "Now I'll show you another little thing he can do," and giving Baldy's nose a shove with the palm of his hand, he spoke the order quick and sharp: "*Al corral! Anda! Ve-te!*"

As Baldy sprang forward Bodewin struck him on the hip. The horse shot away down the slope from the cabin. Dad looked on contentedly, watching for the next manœuvre; but Tony, already suspicious, was now raging, sure that Bodewin had tricked them and that Baldy was off for camp. The horse was nearly a hundred yards away, going at full speed, when Tony fired at him between the tree-trunks once and missed him;

twice — he did not stop; a third shot would have been useless.

Tony turned to Bodewin, with his smoking pistol in his hand.

"That's your racket, is it? You've sent that horse to town."

Bodewin looked white and ugly.

"He'll just tell them I got your papers, that's all," he said.

"You oughtn't to 'a' fired, Tony," said Dad. "I believe you hit him. A bullet-hole won't look well onto him."

"I wish to —— I'd killed him! They'll be scourin' the whole country."

"You're mighty right." Then turning to Bodewin, Dad said, "Mr. Bodewin, you'll have to be kep' pretty clost for a few days."

"All right," Bodewin replied. "By the way, what am I to call you? You introduced yourself, but you didn't mention your name."

"My name — well — it's — Jim — Jim Keesner."

"Thank you, Mr. Keesner."

The door opened, and Babe, still flustered, but shy-eyed and lofty, called them in to supper.

CHAPTER XV.

CIRCUMSTANTIAL EVIDENCE.

EARLY on the morning after Bodewin's disappearance a telegram from Mr. Craig was received at the mine, asking news of Bodewin. Two men had already set out from the camp to search the trail for signs which might lead to some conclusion as to what had become of him. None were found, nor was there evidence of any kind indicating a struggle by the wayside. Various theories were advanced as to Bodewin's fate, but the general opinion in the camp, in view of his known reluctance to appear on the trial, was what he himself had expected it would be. The pistol-mark on Baldy's hip was pronounced, by experts in such matters, the work of a hand that had been careful not to aim too well — probably the hand of Baldy's master. If Bodewin had been stopped on the road by persons who had reasons for not wishing their business with him to be known, they would never have allowed his horse to escape, especially with that mark upon him. So said the men of experience. That any such persons would have allowed the horse to get beyond range of a dead-sure shot was too wild an improbability altogether. Bodewin, no doubt, was hiding out until after the trial, and had sent Baldy home with a blood-stain on him to lead conjecture astray.

In these days Josephine felt strongly drawn towards Hillbury. She saw him frequently, but he never spoke to her of Bodewin, even when the latter's disappearance was the one topic in the camp, and she believed that his silence, like her own, covered a heartache to which words could give no relief. Hillbury was no less drawn towards Josephine. She was more beautiful than ever, he thought. She had the look of one who was suffering. He would have been glad to believe it was not for Bodewin's sake — from no reason personal to himself, — so he assured himself, — but from a lamentable suspicion, that cut him very deep on the score of friendship, that Bodewin was unworthy. Hillbury was not yet willing to believe him so, but the doubt was in itself a trouble. It was also a responsibility, for while he harbored it he felt like a traitor to his friend; yet he could not free himself from it.

A few days before Bodewin took his ride up the pass, Hillbury had made a second search for the mysterious cabin. He had found it, and there began his sadness. He had come upon it as unexpectedly as if it had sprung up out of the earth. Some accident of the location had the curious effect to render it invisible from any point of view that was not very near. There was no one at home, or so Hillbury supposed. Finding himself out of matches and in urgent want of a smoke, he pushed open the door, after the unceremonious fashion of the region, and looked about within for what he required. He had expected to find a match or two without any trouble, then quietly to go his ways and pass on his obligation to some other needy wayfarer. But the matches were not in any of the usual places. He found them at last in an Indian basket of braided grasses, made in the shape of half a hollow sphere, that rocked when he touched it, on the corner of a high wooden shelf. Poking about in it for a match with a buckskin glove on, he upset it and spilled its contents on the floor, — sewing materials, a woman's thimble, the matches, an imperfect pack of cards, one of them cut as for the measure of a hem or tuck, and — a photograph of John Bodewin! An old and faded picture of him in his cavalry uniform, slim in figure, with the boyish face fixed in that slightly exaggerated look of determination which characterized the pictures of our young volunteers. The mustache was faintly perceptible, the hair a little longer than Bodewin's present cut, but it was Bodewin without the shadow of a doubt. Hillbury was touched at seeing the face of his friend as he had known it fifteen years before; it sobered him with a rush of recollections; and then came the cold conjecture, how should it be there — in the cabin which Bodewin had declared was purely of Craig's invention? Hillbury hated mysteries. He wished his friends' lives to be, like his own, in no need of explanation or defence. Here was something to be accounted for. While he stood musing, with the picture in his hand, the outer door of the cabin was pushed open, and a girl, bareheaded, carrying an apronful of pine chips, entered the room. Hillbury was not as surprised to see her as she evidently was to see him. He had recognized her at once as the girl of Craig's adventure. He apologized for his intrusion. The girl had let fall her apron-load on the hearth, and stood as if waiting for him to take his departure. Her beauty corresponded to Craig's description better than her *manner*. That "sweet, stolid way" he had spoken of was not conspicuous to Hillbury's notice. At that moment, certainly, she looked neither sweet nor stolid, but rather keenly and resentfully observant of her visitor. There was in Hillbury's manner a certain superiority, as a matter of course, which his equals admitted and even liked, if he happened to like them, but which his inferiors, socially speaking, were apt to find as uncompanionable as a "no trespass" on a signboard. Hillbury appreciated the girl's beauty, in the abstract, as he would have appreciated the beauty of a perfect crystal; as a woman, she had no existence for him, and, as a woman, she instantly felt it.

"Pardon me," said Hillbury, suddenly aware that he was still holding the photograph. "Is this a picture of a friend of yours?"

"No," said the girl. She seemed to hesitate, and then added, "not to say a friend."

Hillbury could not help seeing that she was blushing, and that some excitement made her breath come deep and short. It might be anger, but it did not look like it.

"Is it — pardon me again — a friend of your father's?" The girl did not reply, and Hillbury added, "I take the liberty of asking because it is a picture of a friend of mine, and I cannot help being surprised to find it here."

Hillbury could not help laying a slight emphasis on the last word. The girl's color deepened as she said, "I do' know as you had any call *to* find it here."

"Very true," Hillbury admitted, smiling in acknowledgment of the just retort; "but you see I have found it, as it happens, and really I would like to know how it came here."

"Well, then, I can't tell you."

"Do you mean you cannot tell me because you do not know?"

"I mean you needn't ask me no more questions, for I won't answer 'em."

"Very well," said Hillbury; "here is the picture, and here is my card. When you see this gentleman again, please hand it to him, will you?"

The girl took the picture and the card he gave her. She looked doubtfully at the words, " U. S.

Geological Survey," engraved beneath the name.
They conveyed to her mind no idea beyond that
vague suspicion with which the passwords of the
educated class are regarded by the ignorant. She
was not sure that this easy yet distant stranger
was not making her in some way the instrument
of his diversion — perhaps at her own expense.

Hillbury stood in the doorway, watching her
with puzzled, unhappy interest. Her beauty, as
of a perfect young animal, a triumphant survival
of the fittest feminine type, impressed him the
more as he examined it. She was as handsome as
Josephine, and as much more dangerous, to the
average man, as passion without discipline could
make her.

The girl found nothing to reassure her in Hillbury's inscrutable dark eyes. He lifted his hat
and gravely wished her good-afternoon, and again
his courtesy seemed to remind her of the distance
between them.

Hillbury had a great fondness for Bodewin.
He was quite used to disapproving of him. He
was always longing to put him to rights, to rouse
his ambition, and make him show for what he was
worth. But, illogical as Bodewin's life was, in his
friend's opinion, and provoking as were his habits,

Hillbury had ever found him one of the most truthful, sensitive, and scrupulous of men. Yet he was aware that there was a side of Bodewin's life he knew nothing of. There had been a journey to Deadwood to which Bodewin had never referred, though it was evident to all who knew him that, in one way or another, it had been a hard trip for him; and there was this trouble with Harkins which Bodewin had gloomily alluded to. Why not go to him frankly and ask him what all this nonsense was about, and what, in particular, he meant by pretending ignorance of a house where a discussion of his picture called up so much feeling on the part of a pretty resident? Decidedly that was the proper thing to do. Since he had spoken *of* Bodewin in the matter, he could do no less than speak *to* him. He would open the subject on the first suitable occasion. No such occasion came, however. It seemed almost as if Bodewin might be trying to avoid him. Hillbury did not see him again to speak with him before his departure for Denver.

Hillbury had certain convictions which he never expressed, because they were incapable of proof. One of these was the conviction that Bodewin was not dead. About two weeks after Bodewin's disappearance, when all efforts to find him or to learn his fate had ceased in the camp, Hillbury set out one day alone in search of his friend. He had mentioned to no one the object of his journey. He took the same way by which he had guided Mrs. Craig's party to the lake. He passed the burnt timber, entered the spruce forest, and, plodding on through gleam and shadow, kept the trail as far as a certain ridge which he followed, moving now more slowly and looking about him for that little hollow where the cabin lurked, and where he expected to find, yet hoped not to find, his friend.

He came upon the cabin from the rear, and finding the ground around the prospect-hole unsuitable for a nearer approach on horseback, he dismounted, and walked around the cabin towards its entrance. He could see the porch while he was still some distance from it, — the long bench, sheltered by the projecting roof, — and seated there, conspicuous in the morning sunlight, he saw John Bodewin. His back was partly turned to Hillbury. Against his shoulder rested a woman's head, a young head, thickly covered with light, shining hair. His hand seemed to press it closer, while his head was bent over the face beneath his own. An idyllic stillness and peace surrounded the solitary cabin. There seemed no one in the forest but these two silent, lover-like figures — and Hillbury, who had set his foot within their paradise. Hillbury did not see a man seated, smoking, on the farther end of the bench, where a hop vine sheltered it. He looked but an instant upon what he believed to be his friend's disgrace, and then tramped fiercely back to the spot where he had left his horse.

As he rode homeward through the melancholy spruces, his hot disgust passed, and left a feeling as if he had come from a burial. "I knew he was not dead. Would that he were — would that he were, rather than this!" He lay sleepless in his blankets that night before his camp-fire, going over and over again the evidence against Bodewin, and trying to find some flaw in the chain of proofs.

He remembered that Bodewin had not joined in the mirth over Craig's story of the cabin and the pretty, golden-haired girl who had said she was a stranger in those parts. He had declared there was no such cabin. He had afterwards seemed to waver and half withdraw the assertion. The cabin had been found, and his picture had

been seen there. The girl had blushed, and refused to talk of it or of him. He had refused to
go on the Eagle Bird case because of some mysterious hold Harkins had on him through a woman.
He had been on the verge of a confession, or an
explanation, which was evidently painful to him.
He had at the last moment consented to give his
testimony, had declined to go over the range with
the Eagle Bird outfit, had gone alone, and had
not been heard from since. He was at the cabin
in the woods, the cabin he had pretended to doubt
the existence of, comfortably secluded, in the
society of a handsome girl, of a class from which
he could not take a wife.

Would that he were dead! Hillbury summed
up the case against his friend. The sad, pure,
sensitive Bodewin, negligent, yet over-scrupulous,
whom he had loved and watched over for many
years, was no more, — nor had he ever been. The
poor fellow had his own strange charm. Hillbury
owned it and missed it, even then when he believed that he had long been misled by it. The
next evening he went to see Josephine. He went
more than once to see her; nor could he yet assure
himself that she was not grieving silently for
Bodewin. One evening he asked her if she would

take a ride with him in the valley. She turned red and then pale.

"No," she said; "I hate the valley!"

"Wherever else you please, then."

"No, not anywhere, thank you. I shall not ride any more while I am here."

When he went home that night, he said to himself, "She, too, is mourning for the living dead." And when he considered how her thoughts must be dwelling on the recreant Bodewin and idealizing him in his absence, the folly of his friend's conduct seemed to him almost more tragic than its baseness.

CHAPTER XVI.

BABE.

THE Keesner cabin consisted of two rooms, one behind the other, with an unfinished loft above them. The rear room was built into the hill, windowless, and lighted only from the adjoining room. Babe had slept in this part of the cabin, called the "dug-out," until Bodewin became one of the family, when it was given to him, and Babe took the garret for her bedroom.

The Keesners, father and son, slept below in the outer room, across the doorway of Bodewin's room. They lay, with their guns beside them, on a camp blanket sewed to the hem of the calico curtain which covered the doorway. The blanket was an extension of the curtain; sleeping on it, they were thus in a position to be disturbed by any movement of it from within.

At five o'clock on the morning after his capture, Bodewin and his keepers were still asleep. The interior of the cabin was dim and quiet as the gray morning twilight in the woods outside. Babe had been softly moving about overhead, and now she came down the ladder which, propped against a square hole in the floor of the garret, served for a staircase. A few red coals were still winking among the ashes· on the hearth. She raked them out, and started a blaze with kindlings laid ready overnight. Then she took the water-pail, and went out to fill it at the well. By this time, her father and brother were awake. They got up with a noise of boots like horses waking in their stalls, and limped, grumbling and cursing, to the fire.

"Floor gits mighty cold, nights," said the elder Keesner. "Dum nigh par'lized!" he muttered, rubbing his chilled joints. Tony, squatting on the hearth, shoulders drawn together, and hands spread to the warmth, spat into the ashes in silence.

Bodewin now came out and asked for water to wash with. Neither of the men stirred, but Dad said : —

"Guess Babe ain't done with the basin yet."

Tony, on reflection, went to the door and ordered her to hurry up, and was in turn ordered by his father to "shut that door!"

In a few moments Babe came in, looking pink about the ears and elbows, with damp rings of hair standing out around her forehead, and offered to Bodewin a clean bright tin basin, which had been not only emptied but wiped. She filled it for him as he held it, gave him a coarse clean towel and a square of yellow soap; but not a glance or a word did she bestow upon him.

" 'Tain't often Babe's mad lasts overnight," her father remarked as she left the room.

When Bodewin, his camp toilet completed, went to the door to empty the tin basin, he was fain to linger there a moment for another look at Babe. She was hanging out the blankets to air, standing a little way off, in the clear morning sunlight, against the bronze and green tones of the forest distance. Her attitude, with both arms lifted, showed the nymph-like proportions of her form. From the back-thrown head, and full short curve of the chin melting into the long white curve of the throat, to the strong-springing line of her instep, that lightly upbore her to her fullest height, she was to the eye perfect.

Bodewin prudently reflected that her speech would probably be disillusioning. Dad Keesner and Tony had followed him closely with their rifles in their hands. He turned suddenly from the open door and confronted them, glancing coolly from their faces to their weapons.

"You don't need to go to that door again," said Dad; and Tony added, "We kin empty your slops for you."

At breakfast the three men sat down together, and Babe waited on them. Bodewin thought of those long-haired, white-armed northern captives serving in the tents of their conquerors. Babe's beauty had in it the element of tragedy, as he discovered when he tried to find her prototype in romance or tradition.

During the next three days Bodewin was confined to the cabin, Dad and Tony relieving each other in the close watch they kept upon him. He saw much of Babe, as she went and came about her housework, but he was far too wise in the ways of all proud, shy, dependent creatures to force himself in the slightest upon her notice. He was tolerably sure that he was observed, and that keenly, but he was not impatient to learn the nature of Babe's conclusions with regard to himself. In small, unobtrusive ways he made himself useful to her, but most of the time he was occupied with mild resources of his own to which she was a stranger. He made sketches in his note-book. Happening to have about him a stylo-graphic pen charged with ink, he took advantage of its unexpected fluency, and copied some strag-gling pencil-notes from one book into another. This latter amusement, however, aroused the sus-picions of his keepers. Keesner remarked that there wasn't any post-office anywhere in that part of the woods, and that he guessed Bodewin's let-ters could wait.

Bodewin took the hint good-humoredly enough. It was part of the situation which he had decided to accept. But afterwards, as he sat smoking by the fire, his occupation gone, his face fell into its habitual expression, a sadness which bore no refer-ence to his present circumstances, but was rather an aggregation dating from the time of his moody boyhood. Babe, looking at him wistfully, and forgetting in his evident abstraction to ignore his presence in the room, interpreted it otherwise. Bodewin, having nothing else to do, continued to smoke, and to stare at the water which was begin-ning to ruffle in a saucepan propped on two stones above a bed of coals. Babe had gone out of doors. Shortly she returned with something that moved, bundled in her apron. She came over to the hearth, knelt in front of Bodewin, and lowering her arms showed him a young setter dog, that immediately began whirling about in her lap and caressing her hands and face alternately. She muzzled his nose with both hands.

"Pretty, ain't he?" she asked, smiling down into the creature's face, and trying to fix his soft, restless brown eyes with her own. The dog snuffed and. struggled, and tried to free his nose from the pressure of her circling fingers. Bodewin leaned down and admired him, pulling his ears, looking at his teeth, and inquiring his age and name.

"We call him 'Pardner,'" Babe replied to the last question. "Don't you want him to play with? He's heaps of company."

The dog was transferred from Babe's lap to Bodewin's knees. As Pardner objected to the smell of tobacco, Bodewin put his pipe in his pocket. Babe stood up, and for a moment lost her shyness of Bodewin in the fond content with which she regarded his wooing of her pet. She remonstrated with Pardner for chewing Bodewin's sleeve-buttons, but evidently thought no less of Bodewin for holding his ornaments so cheap, or the dog so dear.

"You can fool with him all you want to," she said finally. "He don't belong to anybody in this house but me."

After these first few days of confinement Bodewin was allowed to spend his time as he preferred, either in the cabin or outside in the woods, close by. One day Tony was missing, and the next morning Jim Keesner volunteered that Tony had heard from the camp yesterday. The Eagle Bird had obtained a postponement of the trial for a month, — "on account of unavoidable absence of principal witness," Keesner quoted complacently. He then made Bodewin the offer of his liberty, on condition that he would swear not to testify on this or any subsequent trial of the case between the two mines, and that he would keep the secret of his abduction. Bodewin smiled at this proposition.

Keesner admitted that he had not expected him to accept it, and advised him to take his detention as coolly as possible, since it would now necessarily be prolonged until after the trial.

Keesner protested that neither he nor Tony had anything against Bodewin, unless it might be Tony "owed him one on that circus with the horse." And further, he was willing Bodewin should know that, "although *they* hel' the cards, *Harkins* was runnin' the game."

While they were on the subject Bodewin asked if it was not Harkins who had planned his capture.

Keesner shut one eye tight and fixed the other on the toe of his uppermost boot, as he sat, with his knees crossed, on the bench by the door. "That there Harkins is jest murmurin' h——— when he gits started! He's jest omnivorous!" He rocked himself forward on his crossed arms and laughed with deep and silent enjoyment.

"How did he know I was going alone by the trail?" Bodewin asked.

"How does Harkins know anything! If you'd 'a' went the other way he'd been fixed for you just the same. How'd he git your picture?"

"What!"

Keesner rose up chuckling and went into the cabin, followed by the roused look of inquiry in Bodewin's eyes. He fumbled about on the mantelshelf, and came back with a photograph, which he laid on Bodewin's knee.

"There ye are! How'd he git that?"

Bodewin stared at the picture in gloomy amazement. He had not seen it since the day, fourteen years ago, when he stood by the white-draped table in his sister's room at home, talking to her of Frank Eustis, his eyes meanwhile wandering absently from one to another of her innocent girlish trophies. It was the day before Frank Eustis came, at his invitation, on that hapless visit. So all these years of their separation she had kept her brother's picture. Seldom as she might have looked upon it, there must have been some lingering sentiment which had prevented her from parting with it. Bodewin was at no loss to guess how, among her poor belongings, it had passed from the hand of Harkins's lady friend to Harkins himself, to be finally put to this ingenious use. Harkins had certainly a devilish sense of humor.

"Why did Harkins give you this, do you know?" Bodewin asked at length.

"So we wouldn't miss our man," Keesner replied. "I never set eyes on you, and didn't want to, beforehand, — see, — for fear you'd know me when I come to tackle you on the road."

Bodewin tore up the picture, Keesner looking on and making no objection. It had served its purpose, so far as he was concerned.

It had served another purpose. The picture had been sent to the cabin a month or more before

Bodewin himself was brought there. Babe had not seen many pictures in her life. She had never known a man's face like the one this picture set before her. Poring over it whenever she could have it to herself unobserved, there had been time enough for the sowing of those seeds of trouble which were now maturing fast.

So, while Tony sulked and Bodewin rested in his brief exemption from responsibility, and Keesner chuckled over Harkins's cleverness and counted the wages of his own iniquity, Babe was the common victim.

CHAPTER XVII

AMATEUR SURGERY.

THAT evening by candle-light in the cabin Bodewin was looking over a collection of "specimens" which represented the financial hopes and disappointments of the Keesner family for the past two or three years. Jim Keesner was trying to get a professional opinion from Bodewin regarding a certain piece of quartz he had at that time a particular interest in. It had been taken from one of Keesner's numerous "prospects" which Harkins had just bonded for ten thousand dollars. Bodewin's safe-keeping until after the trial had a more important bearing on the sale of Keesner's mine than the value of the property itself.

Keesner was well aware of this fact; but there was the bare possibility that the mine might be worth something like the amount of the bond, in which case Harkins's bounty on Bodewin's capture and detention would not amount to much after all. Highly as Keesner respected his principal's ability, he did not care to furnish an illustration of it in his own person. It was a privilege to be associated in business with a man like Harkins; nevertheless it was a privilege one might at any moment be called upon to pay dearly for.

Bodewin turned the quartz specimen over on his palm and tried its weight. In order to obtain a fresh fracture he struck it, as it lay on his open hand, with another piece of stone he had picked up from the table. As the quartz fell in pieces, Babe, who had been leaning over Tony's shoulder, looking on at the inspection of minerals, drew back quickly. She had got a particle of the sharp quartz sand in her eye.

She went away from the light and sat apart with her hand over her face, refusing to have the eye looked at. Her father teased her, and Tony bullied her with various methods of extracting the sand. Babe would have none of them, and finally went to bed, saying "it would work out itself before morning."

She came down early as usual next day and prepared breakfast, making no complaint. She had tied a bandage over the injured eye, and was

evidently suffering, though still obstinate when
remedies were suggested. After breakfast Tony
went to the corral to feed the horses. Dad Keesner had taken his favorite seat for a morning
smoke, on the corner of the bench sheltered by a
hop-vine, and near the cabin window. He could
thus enjoy the still September sunshine and keep
at the same time an eye on Bodewin, who sat
within, whittling, by the hearth. Babe had
washed and put away her breakfast things,
moving about silently, as she had done ever
since the formidable stranger's arrival. She now
took down the broom from its nail behind the
door, a sign that she wanted the cabin cleared of
men.

Bodewin had been at work on a couple of
match-sticks, whittling them until each one was
as soft and thin at the end as a fine, flat camel's-
hair brush. With these frivolous-looking imple-
ments in his fingers he approached Babe and said
gently, but as if he expected her to listen : —

"I want to take that thing out of your eye. It
is time it was out."

"How are you going to ?" Babe asked.

"Come here to the light, and I will show you."

As she hesitated, Bodewin took the broom out

of her hands, keeping his eyes upon her and motioned towards the door. He waited for her to precede him, grave, courteous, but peremptory as a physician should be.

She obeyed, laughing a little nervously, perhaps at the novelty of finding herself obedient to masculine direction.

At his command she sat down on the bench outside. turning her face to the right.

"Take off the bandage, please."

She took it off with fingers that were slightly tremulous. Bodewin gave her one of the match-sticks and showed her how to moisten the whittled 'end in her mouth, until it was soft and pliable as a feather. Then taking her head firmly against his shoulder he pressed her shrinking lids apart, and passed the slip of wood under the lid, from the outer to the inner corner of the eye.

The relief was instantaneous. Babe's head drooped. Helpless tears bathed her cheek where the mounting blood was fast effacing the impress of Bodewin's fingers.

He did not look at her at once, but turning to her father, showed him the speck of quartz on the soft end of the stick he had just used.

"— Hisht!" said Keesner, taking his pipe from

his mouth. "Tony!" he called, leaning to look past Bodewin. "Is that you, Tony? I thought I heered a man's feet goin' round the house. Did you hear him?" turning to Bodewin.

"Yes, I heard it; I thought it was Tony," Bodewin replied.

Keesner listened a moment, dubiously, and then resumed his pipe. There was nothing surprising in the silence that had followed Keesner's call. Tony rarely condescended to raise his voice in answer to the paternal summons, but made his appearance in due time when it pleased him to come.

Bodewin, meantime, in whom captivity' had bred a habit of restlessness that was not natural to him, had wandered back into the cabin, because he was' tired of the porch. He was surprised to see Babe seated by the table, her head bowed low, her face hidden on her crossed arms. He stopped beside her and asked if the wounded eye still gave her pain. She seemed to repel his sympathy by a mute gesture which left him still in doubt as to the cause of her trouble.

"What is it, Babe? What is the matter?" he urged.

Babe had never in her life listened to a man's

voice like Bodewin's, with sensitive inflections, that made her color come and go, and a distinctive quality like that of a musical instrument. His low tones touched her the more keenly now by contrast to that peremptory manner of the physician he had before assumed. They thrilled across her fresh, wild sensibilities as the tenderest uttered words might have done. She raised her head and looked up at Bodewin without speaking. Bodewin turned away. He was impatient of this uncalled-for show of feeling in Babe, which seemed to threaten complications in their enforced relation to each other. He was himself intensely, often savagely, preoccupied with thoughts of all that might be doing or done with and finished in that world of his own, from which he had been eliminated as by death. It was irritating to have to think about Babe when he wanted to think about himself. He called it thinking about himself when he dreamed restlessly, in the long, silent hours, of Josephine. He would have had this other girl come and go before his absent gaze in her beauty that was so satisfying in its strength and completeness, and be no more of a problem than the sunlight on the wall.

From some impulse, perhaps to satisfy himself that he had not been making too much of a momentary impression, he went back to where Babe still sat, with her face hidden in her hands.

"Let me see that eye again," he said, resuming the matter-of-fact tone of her physician.

"You don't need to; it's all right," she protested, shrinking away from him.

"Let me see it!" he repeated, authoritatively. "It cannot be all right if you have to keep it covered like that."

She let her hands fall and submitted to his scrutiny, but it was impossible to meet his eyes, with such a helpless quivering of her lips, and the blood rushing into her face. She drew back, with a quick, gasping sigh, and burst into tears.

"What are you crying about?" said Bodewin, angry with himself, and with Babe for making him feel both foolish and cruel. "Are you crying because the speck is gone? You will have to forgive me; I cannot put it back again."

During the rest of the day Bodewin made it easy for Babe to avoid him, by keeping outside of the cabin himself. At dinner she did not sit at the table with the family. Bodewin was not surprised at her absence. He knew that she had not forgiven him; moreover, he had observed that Babe would never eat with him if she could help it, partly from shyness, partly from pride. She was intensely sure that in a hundred unknown ways he found her different from the women he was used to. Not to exhibit this difference, she took pains to give him as little of her speech and manners as possible. She had got a step beyond the men of her family, who saw between Bodewin and themselves few differences that were not in their own favor.

At dusk Bodewin found himself alone with Babe a moment in the cabin. Tony sat in the doorway, his rifle between his knees, his face turned towards the copper-colored sunset, glowing behind the woods. It was Tony's watch. Dad was relaxing himself with a twilight stroll outside.

Babe had taken this opportunity to give Bodewin the card which Hillbury had left for him.

"Where did this come from?" Bodewin asked.

"He told me to give it to you."

"He? What, this man?" pointing to the card. Babe looked bewildered.

"I don't know. He was a dark-complexioned man in buckskin clothes. He stopped in here for some matches. There wasn't anybody 'round but me. I found him standing there with your — with that picture of you in his hand."

"And then —?" said Bodewin, seeing the whole situation, and now painfully interested.

"He asked me some questions."

"Do you remember what questions?"

Babe repeated the questions, falteringly, though she remembered them well.

"And you did not tell him I had never been to the cabin, and you had never seen me before?"

Babe was silent.

"This is the worst yet!" Bodewin groaned.

"Tell him yourself when you see him again, if you're so 'shamed of it!" Babe whispered passionately.

"Yes, when I see him again," Bodewin repeated. "When will that be?"

"Sooner than you think, maybe."

"The sooner the better," he said. Stepping back from the hearth, he trod on Pardner's foot. The dog howled dismally, and Babe, with a look of angry reproach at Bodewin, swept the wailing puppy into her arms and carried him out of doors.

When she had prepared supper, she set a single candle in a japanned tin candlestick on the table, and, without speaking to any one, went out into the darkness, leaving the men to themselves.

"What ails Babe?" Tony asked.

"She's on her ear about somethin' or other," her father explained, between large mouthfuls of beans.

"I'd make her quit her foolishness if I was you," said Tony.

"Yes, you better try a lasso to her; maybe you'll fetch her same's you did that there white-faced hoss o' his'n," said the father, winking at Bodewin and laughing uproariously at his own joke.

Bodewin ate his supper in silence and went to bed early. He was not fond of the "dug-out," but its cave-like darkness and stillness suited him to-night better than the society and candle-light of the outer room.

Hillbury's tacit message by the hand of Babe had given him a bad turn. He could not have known that the keen eyes of his friend had surprised Babe's miserable little secret in her face, and that the man of evidence had for once allowed himself to come to a conclusion without

waiting for proof, but without going this length
in his apprehensions, there were reasons enough
why he should be impatient to explain himself.
Small effort as he had ever made to gain it,
Bodewin really hungered for Hillbury's cold and
tardy approbation. His friend's whole attitude
and humor suited him exquisitely in a man; in a
woman the effect might be a little meagre. A
man should never make a fool of himself, but a
woman might do so very charmingly, on occasion,
with the right person, of course.

The conjunction of ideas was hardly complimen-
tary, but Bodewin's next thought was of Josephine. There comes a time, no doubt, in a man's
relations with an attractive woman, when he may
yet decide either to take in sail, emotionally
speaking, or square away before it, trusting there
may be no danger ahead. This time came to
Bodewin about the period of those long gallops
in the valley and pacings homeward through the
pine woods at sunset. Setting his estimate of his
own person, attainments, fortune, and prospects
against her youth, beauty, and nobleness of character, he had decided to take in sail. Theoretically he had begun to do so before his abduction.
It might be questioned how well he would have

succeeded in practice had he been left to complete his journey to Denver, and to return with the honors of chief witness on the winning side, to be petted by the Eagle Bird constituency. As it had turned out, Bodewin more than once since his sequestration had sadly congratulated himself on this stroke of fate which had put him out of temptation's way.

But to-night, in the general upheaval, reason could make no headway against the keen and passionate sense of loss with which he counted the days of his absence. After the trial the Newbolds would probably go East at once; he might never see Josephine again. The break was intolerably sudden. There were things he must say to her before they parted finally. He must clear himself from all injurious, vague suspicions, and establish his good faith in her eyes; then perhaps he might be able to give her up without this clamorous, childish pain.

Bodewin was not the only watcher in the cabin that night. Babe had also gone early to bed, but not to sleep. She had taken Bodewin's last words to her pillow. "The sooner the better," she repeated to herself. It should be soon. It must be soon, for her own sake, if not for his.

She heard her father talking with Tony in the room below. Their voices were slightly lowered, as if the conversation had taken a confidential tone. Babe got out of bed, stepped softly across the loose boards of the floor to the open ladder-hole, and laid herself down beside it. She had come to a bitter, costly resolve with regard to Bodewin, but to carry it out she must learn all she could of her father's intentions towards his prisoner.

Tony was speaking now. "Say, do you know what the talk is down to camp?"

"What do I know about camp!" Dad crossly rejoined. "Hain't seen so much as the sign on a gin-mill for six months."

"There's a heap of talk about *him*. They 'low down there he never would 'a' started if it hadn't 'a' been for Newbold's daughter."

"Say Newbold's coin, and you'll be talkin'."

"Same thing" — it was Tony who spoke again. "Newbold gits his case, and *he* gits the girl, and the coin too. That's what they're talkin' down below."

"Thought you said 'twas ginerally 'lowed he'd lit out by himself, on purpose?"

"That's Sammis's racket. Sammis makes him-

self a heap of importance 'bout now. He knowed
it all beforehand. *He* told 'em just how 'twould
be!"

"Well, it don't look onlikely," said Dad, slowly.

"What don't?"

"That there story 'bout the girl."

"Guess you'd think so if you was to see her
once!"

"Where'd *you* ever see her?"

Babe could not see the men, as they crouched
forward over the fire, but by their shadows
thrown on the opposite wall she could guess at
Tony's attitude.

"I looked at her," he said, leaning towards
his father, without taking his elbows off his
knees, "straight as I'm lookin' at you now, for
much as half an hour up here on Mike's claim.
I could tell you her p'ints like I could Babe's
here."

"She's got p'ints, eh?"

Tony nodded his head, and his giant double on
the wall repeated the action impressively.

"What age 'bout?" Dad asked.

"'Bout Babe's age — little older, maybe. She's
a different color to Babe. Black eyes, and eye-
brows like a streak o' charcoal."

"Sho, I bet she can't hold half a candle to our Babe!"

"I bet she can hold two — ask Bod'in!"

"Durn'd if it ain't a reg'lar circus!"   Dad laughed his low-bred, cunning laugh and slapped his knees.

"Can't ye make a little more noise?" Tony whispered savagely.

"Say, Tony!" — Keesner gave his son a shove with his elbow, — "was he 'long of her up there on the Mike?"

"They was jawin' together, I tell you, the whole durned time. Him a-layin' on his elbow lookin' at her, and her face as red as that coal."

"No!   'Twas the sun likely."

"I tell you, he's dead gone on her.   It's all the talk down to camp.   She put him up to testifyin'. Harkins must 'a' had that in his head when he told us to say she sent the papers."

"That there Harkins is a reg'lar coon," said Dad, with feeling.

"It's going to be a tough pull on him, hidin' out here for a month.   He'll feel mighty ugly when he gits loose," said Tony.

"Harkins has got to settle that bill," Dad replied.   "'Tain't none of my funeral!"

" *You'll* see 'fore we git through whose funeral it will be."

Babe had writhed herself over, prone on the floor, in the darkness. She had no words, no thoughts. She seemed made of one great agony. Nothing was clear to her but the image of Bodewin, his attitude, his eyes. She could feel them resting upon her face as if she had been that other girl whom he was longing to see.

She understood all now, as one sufferer knows another's pain — his restless days, his days of moody silence. The dull, beseeching pain in his eyes meant no want of his that she could satisfy.

Towards morning she got up from the floor and threw herself on her bed. From complete weariness she lost herself, and slept heavily until awakened by her father calling and shaking the ladder below.

CHAPTER XVIII.

ANOTHER OBLIGATION.

THE days of Bodewin's captivity were spent in eating and sleeping, training the setter-pup, arguing with Dad, ignoring Tony, and, over and above his own private fund of sweet and bitter fancy, wondering what could be the matter with Babe. At times, as on the day he had treated the wounded eye, he had fancied he knew what the nature of her trouble was; but the supposition involved such gross and fatuous vanity on his part, that he preferred to reject it, even in the face of symptoms difficult to account for on any other hypothesis.

To keep on the safe side, however, he now spent his days almost entirely out of doors.

He had found some amusement in the making of a rude sun-dial on the top of a pine-stump that had been sawed a few feet from the ground. On its tablet of shaded amber-colored rings he had inscribed the hours in a circle. He was now at work on an appropriate motto, which was to form a lesser circle, inclosing the dial-plate. He had first read it carved on a stone dial that had counted the sunny hours in an old mission garden of lower California. A passion-vine had wound itself about the broken column, and fragrantly closed the record. Bodewin had parted its sprays, heavy with purple blossoms, to read the words:

"Coma la sombra, haya la hora."
(As the shadow, flies the hour.)

Many a time since, in times of waiting or on solitary journeys, they had found their way back to his thoughts and left with him their echo of home-sickness.

Bodewin was cutting the last letters of this inscription one day, when Babe, on her way to the well, stopped and watched him at his work, and lingered still, with nothing to say, yet as if she wished to say something. After waiting for her to speak, Bodewin asked rather sentimentally — "You will look at my clock in the forest, some-times, when I am gone, Babe?"

He found it difficult to avoid a half-caressing, half-condescending tone in talking to her. She made him think of those women in Genesis, with perfect bodies, and souls whose history went not back beyond a few generations.

"You want to leave yere mighty bad, don't you?" she asked in a low voice, without looking at him or replying to his speech about the clock.

"I want to get away, of course," Bodewin answered indifferently, and on his guard at once.

"I've been studyin' 'bout a way to help you off. I can't talk now,—after supper maybe, outside."

After supper Bodewin lit his pipe, and strolled out of the cabin, attended by the familiar consciousness that he was watched by one or both of his keepers. It was Dad's watch to-night. Dad was more cunningly vigilant than Tony. He had an air of abstraction when on duty that made his society less of a restraint on the movements of his prisoner. It was thus he kept *en rapport* with Bodewin's varying mood under the pressure of his long waiting. When her evening work was done, Babe came out and sat a little way off from Bodewin on the bench. Dad smoked, and paced slowly up and down the cleared space in front of the cabin. As it grew dusk, only the red spark of his pipe showed where he moved against the gloom of the trees, and the figures of the two who sat on the bench blended with the shadow of the low projecting roof. Tony was sleeping heavily and audibly on the floor of the cabin. From time to time, in his walk, Dad paused opposite the open door, and listened with disgust to the sleeper's breathing, muttering to himself the reproof he was rehearsing for his benefit. Tony was getting slack about his share of the work in hand, and showing, besides, an inclination to resume his habit of drinking. Dad had unpleasant suspicions as to the cause of this early and profound nap.

This was Babe's opportunity. Speaking low, and with thickening heart-beats, she confided to Bodewin her plan for his escape. The possibility that he might hesitate to avail himself of it had not once occurred to her.

"Thank you, Babe," he said. "It is very sweet of you to want to help me; but I am not going, you know."

"You ain't a-going? Don't you want to go?"

"Not in that way."

He heard her stir softly beside him, as if she sighed.

"I been a-studyin', but I can't think of any other way."

"Never mind, Babe; it's awfully good of you,"

he said, in that caressing tone which was a fatality
of his talk with Babe. "I'll have to see it
through, if you can stand having me around."

Babe moved again restlessly beside him. Hope
was stirring in her heart, telling her that perhaps
he was not so eager to get away after all.

"It is a great temptation," he said at last.
"Have you thought what you will say to your
father when he questions you to-morrow?"

"I ain't afraid of Dad. You can believe me, it
will be worse for me if you keep on stayin' here."

"I thought we were getting to be such good
friends, Babe."

Babe was silent a moment. He thought she
was not going to answer, when she said, with an
effort at lightness, "You know you don't care for
me, only to fool with me."

"I care for any girl too much to fool with her.
It was only on your account I hesitated. Heaven
knows I want to get away badly enough. If you
understand the risk you are taking, and are willing to take it for me — "

"I take it for myself," said Babe proudly. "It
suits me to have you go as well as it suits you to
go. You can go to-night, if you've a mind to
keep awake. When you hear me stirrin' 'round

overhead, climb up the logs to a hole in the floor where you'll see a light — "

She was interrupted by Dad's approach. The old man sauntered towards them out of the twilight, knocked the ashes out of his pipe against a post of the porch, and set his heavy foot upon the boards.

"Git in, git in!" he said. "Night's yere, and mornin's comin'."

Tony was still sleeping by the fire. Bodewin had gone to bed, and Babe was stooping over the coals on the hearth to light her candle, when her father signed to her to draw near. He looked at her fixedly a moment as she stood before him, the unlit candle in her hand.

"'Pears to me you and him's gittin' mighty good friends," he said, with a gesture of his head towards the door of Bodewin's room.

Babe winced; but she faced him desperately.

"If you don't want us to be friends, what you keepin' him here for?" she said.

"That's my business. Your business is to look out for yourself. I don't want no gal's foolishness 'round yere. You hear me?"

The girl flushed and then turned white.

"Dad," she almost whispered, meeting her

father's eyes shrinkingly, "send him away. He don't ought to be yere. I can't bear the sight of him."

"It looks like you can't bear the sight of him! It looks a heap like it!" Dad wagged his head sarcastically. "Now look yere, — I'll tell you somethin' you don't want to forgit. He's got his eye on a different piece of goods to what you be."

Babe did not take her eyes from her father's face while he was speaking. She was trembling, and there was a strange, set smile about her mouth.

"You make me feel like I wish I was dead," she said, heavily. She moved a step backwards, and her eyes fell. Something seemed to break up within her; tears came, and hard, choking sobs.

Her father still eyed her sternly, without any movement of relenting towards her; but she found her way into his arms, and clung to him, rubbing her face against his, humbly.

"There, there," said Dad, soothingly, "don't talk no more foolishness."

Babe lifted her head.

"It ain't foolishness. Oh, you'll see! All of Harkins's mines and all his money won't pay you for the trouble he's makin' here. No; not if you love your poor old Babe!"

She sobbed, holding him by the shoulders, and fairly rocking his sturdy bulk in the strength of her despair.

"Girl," Keesner said, holding her off from him to give his severity its full effect, "you're talkin' mighty queer. You're gittin' simple. Now, you hear me; that man stops yere, you understand? It suits me to have him. If you're so durned skeered of his company I can put you where you'll have a chance to git used to men."

Babe wrenched herself out of his grasp.

"Father!" she cried, in a low, wild voice.

"Don't you come a-fatherin' me!" Keesner interrupted, nodding his big head at her. "You git to bed and salt down what I been sayin' to you."

When Babe had gone to her room Keesner filled another pipe and smoked it tranquilly, satisfied that he had done a parent's duty, and more than satisfied with the situation, as he regarded it, between Bodewin and his daughter. Nothing would have suited Keesner better than for Bodewin to "take a hankerin' after our Babe." He was willing to use his daughter, but not to sacrifice her. It was not in Keesner's scheme that

Babe should suffer any but that intangible harm
which would wear out with a few girlish tears and
reproaches. He had gone a little too far, perhaps,
when he had threatened to send her down to her
Aunt Matild', whose husband kept a billiard and
drinking saloon in the camp. Babe must have
known that that was all a joke. He stirred up
Tony with his foot and made him spread down the
camp blankets and fetch in more wood, growling
like a Caliban, while he himself covered the fire
and bolted the outer door.

About one o'clock Bodewin, lying awake and
dressed on his bed, heard cautious footsteps and
movements overhead. When all was quiet again,
he rose, and, groping his way to the corner of the
room, climbed up the logs and crawled through an
opening in the floor above, where two loose boards
had been removed. He found himself close under
the rafters of the garret, and across the wide, low-
eaved chamber he saw through a square window
in the gable the moonlight on the trees outside.
It was a window of but one sash, which had been
taken out. Bodewin stumbled against it in reaching the window. He heard the stir of the night
breeze, and felt its soft suspiration on his face.
Somewhere in the shadowy room Babe was lying,

breathlessly waiting for him to be gone. He dared not speak to her. He looked once toward the white outline of her bed, and with a mute "God bless her" turned his face to the night and liberty. The descent from the window to the ground, seven feet below, was easily made. Moonlight nights had come again. The last one, he remembered most vividly, was when at Josephine's side he had walked his horse through the lights and shadows of the forest trail on their homeward ride from the lake. The moon was setting behind the low hooded cabin which sat with its shadow at its feet. In one of the bright spots of moonlight, between the cabin and the trees, Bodewin was startled to see a woman's figure standing as if waiting for him. Raising her hand with a gesture of silence, she came towards him, and he saw that it was Babe. She had a shawl over her head, which partly concealed her face. Bodewin protested against this needless risk on her part.

"Your horse is saddled ready here at the cor-ral," she said, without heeding his remonstrance.

Again he insisted that she was doing too much for him.

"The critters know me, and you couldn't find the gear," she said.

"Which horse have you given me?"

"The black one; he ain't known yerabouts."

"That was a good thought," said Bodewin. "I'll see that he gets back. Good-bye, Babe."

He held out his hand. She made no movement to take it.

"You've got to promise me something before you go," she said. Her manner was dull and quiet, as it had been for days past.

"I'll make you any promise in the world that I can honestly keep," Bodewin said.

"This here is between you and Harkins, ain't it? You won't make Dad pay for it?"

"I will swear to you, Babe, that I will take no revenge on any one in this house."

"Nor give us away by name?"

"Your name shall never pass my lips, so help me God."

After a pause she added, "Nor my father's, nor Tony's?"

"You may trust me. I will be silent for your sake, remember — for what you are doing for me to-night."

"I ain't a-doin' it for you," she murmured, doggedly, half to herself.

"I may have to explain," Bodewin continued,

"that I was detained by force. I must do that to clear myself from ugly suspicions about my absence, you understand?"

"It makes no odds to me what you say, so's you don't name us to no one, nor tell where you was kep'."

"It shall be so. Now run in, quick. God bless you."

She said nothing, but dropped her head an instant against the horse's neck. Bodewin thought she kissed it. When she had turned away, he mounted and rode on slowly, looking back and only half satisfied to go, while Babe still stood where he had left her, with her head down.

She stood there listening until the last light hoof-tread had died away. She then walked slowly around the cabin to the mound behind it, where the platform of boards glistened frosty in the moonlight. Behind the cabin no one, looking out by chance, could see her if she sat awhile and tried to realize what it was she had done. How would it be when her father came to question her as to Bodewin's escape?

The garret floor, once the boards were laid back in their places, would tell no tales, but a young

girl's countenance is not so safe a shield to put
before a secret. Her heart sank at the thought
of her father's eyes resting on her face, as they
had the night before, when he had scourged her
to bed with his brutal words. The threat, moreover, with which he had dismissed her that night
haunted her with a dread worse than that of any
imaginable death. It was an overmastering fear,
which made the night and the forest seem like
home to her, by comparison with the house where
her father and her brother lay asleep. Where
should she go, along that pathway, wide as the
gate and easy as the way of all desperate journeys? She tried her feet upon it, as it were.
They did not refuse to obey her. She walked
on, hardly aware how far she had gone on
the blind forest track Bodewin had taken before
her.

On a sudden a thought she had dwelt on often
before asserted itself in the dull confusion of her
mind. She would see the face of that other girl
— the dark-eyed, the chosen one. Perhaps she
might have sight of their happiness together.
After that, whatever came to her, it would be easy
to bear.

The resolve nerved her with sudden strength.

She walked on fast, with long, soundless steps. Her head felt clear. Her journey had now an object. By daybreak she would be on the edge of the forest; and then, by the nearest and loneliest trail, she would find her way to the Eagle Bird mine.

CHAPTER XIX.

THE PRICE OF BODEWIN'S LIBERTY.

It was evening of the day of Bodewin's return. All that afternoon in Mr. Craig's office he had been in earnest consultation with Mr. Newbold and his lawyer concerning the part he was to bear in the coming trial. The consultation had warmed into a discussion which was now closing with some excitement on the part of both lawyer and client. Bodewin was quiet and evidently depressed, but in a new and unexpected direction he was, as Craig would have expressed it, as freaky and mulish as ever. Mr. Craig felt entitled, in his professional capacity, to his witness's full confidence. Bodewin, on the contrary, declined to give any explanation of his late disappearance, beyond the fact that he had been captured on the road and forcibly detained. He carried his reticence to the point of making it a condition of his voluntary presence at the trial, that he should not be questioned as to the place where he had been kept a prisoner, or the authors of his detention. All this mystery was excessively irritating to Mr. Craig.

"Do you suppose I don't know what points to bring out and what to leave alone?" he asked impatiently. "Tell me the whole story, and I will know then what questions to ask you."

"I am not at liberty to tell the whole story to you, Craig, or to any one else," Bodewin replied. He hated to have to explain himself to Craig, whose unfortunate manner always made Bodewin forget that gentleman's numerous good and useful qualities, but it was the only alternative to a prolonged agitation of the subject of his testimony. "You will have to forego the sensation my little adventure might make in court. I was not set at liberty; I got off in the night — but not without help. I don't choose that the first use I make of my freedom shall be to retaliate even indirectly upon those who helped me to it. Harkins was at the bottom of the whole thing, and we will beat him at his own game. It would be childish now to try to revenge ourselves for what is past, on those who are merely his tools. This little episode of my capture has no bearing on the case beyond its showing to what lengths Harkins will go and what risks he will take to make his point. But you would be giving yourself superfluous trouble to show up Harkins. He is well enough known, and so far from prejudicing a jury against him, in my opinion, such a jury as you will be likely to get would be immensely amused by the whole thing, and look at it only as another daring proof of his cleverness. My relations with Harkins are getting somewhat complicated, I'll admit, but they are after all my own affair. If you meddle with them in court, Craig, let me tell you, you'll be sorry for it."

"Confound it, Bodewin, this is the second time you have intimated that you know my business better than I do myself. Perhaps you would like to be witness and counsel both."

Bodewin leaned back in his chair with his hands deep in his pockets, and studied the lacing of his shoes in silence. Mr. Newbold interposed with the assurance that he, for his part, admired Bodewin's magnanimity towards his enemies, and would be the last one to try to overcome his scrupulousness.

"They are not my enemies," Bodewin said.

"Are they your friends?" Craig retorted.

"Come, now, Craig," said Mr. Newbold. "You shall not badger your own witness. Keep that tone for the Uinta men. If Mr. Bodewin is as true to us as he is generous to those fellows who plotted his abduction, we'll have no fault to find with him."

"Thank you, Mr. Newbold, but you give me too much credit," said Bodewin, coldly. "The person or persons concerned in my escape had nothing to do with my capture. As for my truth to you, sir, that means simply my truth to the truth itself, in so far as your case represents it. It means that, or else it means that I am a fool," he added, bitterly.

Mr. Craig glanced at his client, as if to say, You see what an uncomfortable fellow he is, take him any way you like.

Bodewin rose and took up his hat. He was conscious that he had been provoked into saying several extremely foolish things, and was anxious to make his retreat before he said any more.

"I shall stay up at the mine to-night, if Mrs. Sammis can give me a bed," he said, addressing himself to Mr. Newbold; and mentally he resolved that he would remain there until the camp had done asking questions and talking about him. Something new would turn up in a day or two — a suicide, or a street fight, or a stage robbery, or a rich strike of mineral — to divert the public interest from his own affairs.

In the meantime he could get a better grasp over his feelings towards Josephine. It was but a month he had been missed from the little stage of the camp, yet the parts might be all changed. Hillbury and Josephine were perhaps even now riding homewards in the sunset glow, after a long gallop in the valley, as he and Josephine had ridden a month ago. The explanation he had longed to make his friend, as to the photograph •and the cabin, was now impossible through his promise to Babe the night of his escape. His appearance on the witness-stand with Craig as a questioner was seriously complicated by it.

Why under the heavens had he accepted Babe's help? Was he such a fool as to have forgotten that a man cannot take favors from a woman who is fond of him unless he returns her fondness? Is even a month's captivity enough to soften a man's brains as well as his muscles? Dad and Tony's rifles no longer restrained his movements, but he was not a free man. His promise was scarcely

twenty-four hours old, yet already he hated it
worse than he had hated his obligation to Harkins. For it was a promise to a woman, and a
woman whose circumstances, compared with his
own, made her peculiarly helpless. Harkins
could "get even" with him for the slighted
obligation, in his own way; but Babe could take
no reprisals. These thoughts were passing through
his mind while Mr. Newbold was saying, "We
shall be most happy to have you, my dear fellow;
we'll ride up together if you like."

"I beg your pardon," said Bodewin.

"I say, we'll ride up to the mine together, if
you've no objection," Mr. Newbold repeated.

"Are you staying at the mine?" Bodewin asked,
in surprise and some confusion.

"Yes," said Mr. Newbold. "We have given
up our rooms at the Wiltsie. Josephine disliked
the restaurant, and she insists that the Sammises
need the price of our board, especially as Sammis
will probably have to resign. He can't stay, of
course, if the mine goes into Harkins's hand,
though I have suspected that lately he has been
hedging a little; and if we get our case — thanks
to you — I shall want a different man altogether."

Mr. Newbold and Bodewin had left the lawyer's office and were now riding slowly up the street.

"I haven't seen Hillbury yet," Bodewin said. "He must have got into his new quarters by this time?"

"Oh, yes — so he has," said Mr. Newbold, vaguely. "I believe Mr. Hillbury did say something about his rock specimens the other evening. He asked us to come down and look at them now he has them all boxed and arranged."

"How *is* Hillbury?" asked Bodewin.

"Oh, he's all right, I guess. We haven't seen much of him. He came up to the mine once or twice: but to tell you the truth, my dear fellow, we have been a house of mourning since you were spirited away. My daughter has been — well — she's been a little absurd about it, I tell her. She seemed to feel that we were somehow accountable for your fate, because it was on our side you were going to testify. I couldn't feel that way myself, but then women will think of more ingeniously disagreeable things once they get low in their minds—. Josephine is a terrible hand to worry if she thinks she, or any of her family, for that matter, is to *blame* about anything," said Mr. Newbold, feelingly.

This phase of Josephine's melancholy was less sweet to Bodewin than her sorrow would have been, undiluted with self-blame, but it was enough to set his heart at rest, so far as Hillbury was concerned.

As they passed a quiet corner near the assay office, Bodewin saw Hillbury himself standing in the door of the office. At the sight of his friend's face and characteristic pose, guarded and dignified even in its unconsciousness, a tender, half-humorous enjoyment of him swelled in Bodewin's heart. It gave him a certain surprise to find how fond he was of Hillbury. His desire of the moment was to jump off his horse and seize upon Hillbury and assure him, "It is all right about the cabin, all right about the photograph, all right about everything; I cannot explain, but you must have faith in me, old fellow, as I would have in you if things looked queer."

"Hullo, here is Hillbury!" he called out joyously. "I'll catch up with you on the next block," he said to Mr. Newbold, and turned his horse's head sharply towards the sidewalk. Hillbury's eyes kindled at sight of Bodewin's face, and then grew stern.

"How are you, old man?" said Bodewin, reaching a hand to him from his saddle. "You don't look as if you had mourned for me much."

Hillbury's hands were in the side pockets of his coat; he kept them there, regarding Bodewin calmly. Hillbury's habit of repression deceived people as to his emotional capacity. At the moment he was deeply disturbed, but no trace of his inward struggle betrayed itself.

"I have mourned an old friend lately," he said, with a sad dignity of manner that sobered Bodewin at once. "Can you tell me anything about him?"

"Is he a friend of mine?" asked Bodewin, speaking· bewilderedly the first words that came.

"He should be — his name is John Bodewin. I thought I saw him a week ago amusing himself in an idyllic fashion in a cabin in the Lake woods; but as he once assured me there was no such cabin, I must have been mistaken."

Bodewin returned Hillbury's look steadily. "Were you looking for John Bodewin when you saw him as you say?"

"I was."

"Why did you go *there* to look for him? To find out if he was a liar and a scoundrel? I'll tell you where you *were* mistaken, Hillbury — in call-

ing a man you did not trust your friend. When
you begin to suspect your friends, you will not
lack trifles to confirm your suspicions."

" There may be a difference of opinion as to
what are trifles," Hillbury said. Bodewin looked
once more at his friend. His dark eyes softened
into no returning tenderness, though Bodewin's
eyes were smarting with a hot, shameful moisture.
The blow had cut him keenly. It was so unexpected — so coolly, neatly delivered. Misunder-
standings between friends are not always hopeless
things, especially when the friends are men, and
capable of reasoning even upon questions of feeling. But how to come to an explanation with
a man who is convinced that none is needed?
Well, let it go — the friendship that has no foun-
dation in faith is not worth the entreating for.
He had thought it seasoned timber that would
not give, but it had parted with the first strain.
So Bodewin tried to philosophize away his pain;
but it stayed. It gnawed into his self-respect, not
an excessive virtue with Bodewin in his best
moods. It took all the sweet excitement out of
his meeting with Josephine.

CHAPTER XX

A STAR IS HIDDEN.

THE low black aperture of a tunnel facing the valley and the sunset gave entrance to the underground territory of the Eagle Bird. Work was still going on in that portion of the mine not under dispute. All night and all day, at recurrent intervals, the figure of a miner appeared at the tunnel's mouth, pushing a loaded car along the tramway to the dump. He came out at high noon, when the sky glowed incandescent behind the blackened boles of the pine trees, or when the shadow of the range lay half across the valley, or when the shadow had climbed the darkly wooded slopes opposite, and above it the loftiest peaks were entering solemnly into the glory of the sun's down-sinking. The miner was still coming and going, the roll of the car on the iron track was still heard, when the stars twinkled sharply in the long strips of sky between the pine trunks ; and darkness, that all day lurked within the tunnel, stalked forth and possessed the land. The roll of the wheels, the clank of the bolt as the car reared on its axle, and the dull crash of the avalanche of earth and stones that followed, were sounds that could be heard a long way off in the stillness of the wood.

These were the sounds by which Babe knew when she had reached the end of her journey. She heard them first about sunset as she approached the mine by the trail from the pass. She had gone the long way round. Once only she had stopped to rest, at the little ranch at the foot of the pass, where the woman was still baking pies in the outdoor oven for her wayfaring customers. Babe was not a customer. She had merely stopped to ask the way and the number of miles to the Eagle Bird mine, where, she told the woman, she had a brother employed as a miner. Seeing that she looked tired, and mistaking the expression of her face for that of physical suffering, the woman urged Babe to sit and rest awhile, and pressed her kindly to eat and drink. Babe gratefully accepted a glass of cool milk and consented to put in her pocket a piece of bread which she could not force herself to eat. The woman's

questions, and fixed though not unfriendly observation, troubled her, and shortened her rest.
When she came at last within sight and sound of
the mine it was still so light that she did not venture beyond the thin shelter of the wood. She
lay down upon the ground to make herself
less conspicuous. Slowly the shadows crept from
the ground upward to the tree-tops, and a single
star showed in the deepening blue. There were
others in the sky, but this one only Babe looked
at, as with her head low on her arm she rested and
waited for darkness. Presently she saw a light at
the dump station — other lights appeared in windows or moved about among the dark buildings.

The moon was an hour or more high. Babe
started up, aware that she must have fallen asleep
at the foot of the tree where she lay. She returned to the trail by which she had come, and
followed it past the tunnel and up the steep and
dusty path to the high-stooped house built against
the hill, which she had decided must be the dwelling of the superintendent. Here Mr. Newbold's
daughter would be lodged, if she were living at the
mine. Babe made no inquiries to assure herself of
the fact. One or two men (seated on the steps
of the miners' boarding-house) looked at her

curiously as she passed, but she was questioned by no one.

An irregular pile of lumber was stacked close to the side of the superintendent's house; deep shadow filled the space between. Babe crept in over the boards, and climbed to a place where she could look into a bright, uncurtained window of the parlor. The room was empty. A lamp burned on the centre-table and chairs were pushed out of their places. From the sound of voices talking, Babe concluded that the recent occupants of the room were now assembled on the piazza outside. She rose up cautiously and was groping her way forward for a better view, stepping lightly along the tiers of boards, when Bodewin and Josephine came to the end of the porch and leaned side by side on the railing above her. The moon shone full in their faces. Both were gazing upwards, their eyes fixed on one spot in the heavens.

Babe looked up at the same place in the sky, but saw nothing more than the moon, nearly half full, and close to her shadowed side a small, bright star. It was this star Josephine and Bodewin were watching, for from its position that night they knew it must be near its occultation by the moon. As the distance lessened imperceptibly between it and the undefined arc of shadow approaching it, the star seemed to throb and flash, red, gold, and sapphire, as if it were panting to its extinction. If anything could have made those two, standing in the light of heavenly bliss, as it seemed to Babe, more hopelessly far away from her, it was this mysterious, rapt attention fixed upon some object which to her had no existence. At first she thought they might be taking some silent vow together, but then she heard Josephine speaking, in a clear, even voice.

"It is only a little star, but we have looked at it so long it seems the only one in all the sky. Has it a name, do you know?"

"I think it is Antares," Bodewin replied.

"Antares," Josephine replied, dwelling on the vowelled syllable with satisfaction. "The occultation of Antares! How imposing it sounds. And I suppose all the world is watching it with us to-night."

"We are the only watchers in this part of the world, I fancy," said Bodewin,—"except Hillbury, perhaps," he added, sadly. His heart swelled with the pain of love unspoken. Josephine's white-clad shoulder was nearly touching his arm. If he were to put it out and draw her to him it might change both their lives forever. Yes, and it might ruin his. Why should he not speak to her, at least, and take his answer for life or death? There was not an atom of his flesh that did not worship her. And for his better part — who had ever appealed to that as she had done? Had she not found him in a slough of moral doubt and sophistry, and shown him his duty, without question of her right, as if she knew instinctively that she was born to be his soul's mistress and the light of his dull, purposeless life? He was trembling with the intoxicating risk of speech. Josephine's eyes were still upon the star; her hand rested on the rail. The impulse to cover it with his own was so strong that for an instant he fancied he must have done so involuntarily, for suddenly she stepped back and dropped her eyes.

"It is gone!" she said. "Did you see how at the last it seemed to leap out of sight? I am so glad to have seen it; but now let us go in."

"Oh, no, not now; stay until we see it again on the other side." And silently he resolved that before they saw the star again he would know his fate.

"It will not seem like the same star when we see it again," said Josephine; "and if it did it

would only be an anti-climax—like Juliet coming
before the curtain after the death scene."

Her light, cool words confused Bodewin and
gave his passion a moment's check. Josephine
was leaning on her crossed arms gazing down into
the shadow cast by the pile of boards. Some object moving there had attracted her attention.
She had seen a head emerge, as it were, from that
well of darkness — a head framed in moonlight,
the shadowed face invisible. The fair head of a
young woman who crouched among the boards
and looked upwards in a fixed agony of attention.
At the instant Josephine's eyes rested on it, the
head disappeared, but that brief look thrilled her
with the sensation of having long been watched
by some unknown person lurking in the darkness
below.

She turned to Bodewin and said softly, "Look!
who is that?" pointing downwards with her white-
sleeved arm. "You will see her in a moment."
Again the head emerged; this time it was bent and
hidden by a shawl. The moon had climbed a
little higher, and the shadow which had covered
Babe had shrunk away, and left her cowering
form exposed. It had stolen away so gradually
that, absorbed in her unhappy watch, she had not

been aware of its retreat. She was plainly
trapped, with the precipitous bank behind her,
the heap of boards on one side, and bright moonlight illuminating her only way of escape. If she
could gain the trail the dip of the ground would
hide her. She rose up, desperate, and with her
shawl muffling her head and face, walked out into
the light.

Bodewin had not seen the girl's face, and Babe,
a moment before, had been far from his thoughts,
but something within him foreboded that this was
Babe — Babe unhappy and desperate — shelterless,
homeless, perhaps through her service to him.
Surely the figure, the height, the movement were
Babe's as she walked out into the light.

"I think I had better see who that is," he said.
"Excuse me a moment."

If he were to see who it was, there was no time
for ceremony. Josephine watched him down the
steps and across the moonlit space before the slope
of the hill hid him from her sight. She walked
up and down the piazza alone once or twice. She
stood and listened. The dead woods were still.
There were no insect voices calling. It seemed as
if she could almost hear Bodewin's retreating footsteps pounding along down the trail. The rumble

of a car running out from the tunnel drowned the
fainter sounds. The iron rails resounded as the
car travelled swiftly down the track. Was that a
man's voice calling in the woods? Now came the
crash of the car-load over the dump. Why did
they stay so long at the dump-station? She
waited and listened mechanically for the roll of
the returning car-wheels.

Why did Bodewin remain away so long — and
why, in the meantime, was that car still waiting
at the dump-station! She shivered and went
into the house.

Bodewin had caught sight of the figure he was
in chase of as it passed the light at the mouth of
the tunnel. She was running wildly; the shawl
had dropped from her head, and he saw that it
was Babe. Should he let her go? He hesitated;
then his heart smote him for the desolate young
figure flying to the woods for shelter like a
hunted creature. What man has not a tenderness
for the woman he suspects of a hopeless attach-
ment to himself — and Babe must be in trouble.
Perhaps she had come with an intention of asking
his help, and seeing him so preoccupied with
another woman, had in her mad, foolish pride
flung herself away from him into the night and

the forest. She should not go in that way. He had hesitated but an instant, and now followed with greater speed, — down the steep, dim slope of the woods, slipping and stumbling. She was still some distance ahead of him. Now she fell, but was up and on again faster than before. He was close upon her, had called her by name, when she turned and looked back at him, motioned him back with a gesture of her arm, and then, doubling suddenly, she flew along the unused trail across the foot of the dump. It was scarcely wider than a man's two hands. Bodewin heard a car rumbling out from the tunnel — "Babe!" he shouted. "Come back, for God's sake! A car is coming!"

She was nearly half-way across the dump. Bodewin called and waved his arms frantically to the man above. The miner was running behind his car, and the noise of its wheels drowned Bodewin's cries. He started after Babe by the same impossible path she had taken, but at that moment the car reared on its pivot, and the avalanche came. The greater mass of earth clung to the slope of the dump, but stones and pieces of rock leaped and pelted and bounded down the steep. They fell all about Bodewin, but he was not conscious of being hurt. He slid off the trail, and down among the débris below he crawled about, searching for Babe. He found her lying as she had been hurled from the path by the stone that struck her in the breast. He spoke to her as he raised her in his arms and asked if she knew him. She assented with a motion of her head.

"Is there anything you wanted of me, Babe? Tell it me now, if there is, before I go for help."

"I don't want help," she said, speaking with short breaths of pain. "Nobody can help me."

"Don't say that, Babe. Where is your hurt?"

"It don't matter," she panted. "The hurt don't matter. Come closer." She put up her hand to his face. He bent lower to hear her difficult sentences. "Say you won't tell who I am!" she whispered. "Let it be like I was a stranger to you. If Dad finds me out—he'll 'low 't I was followin' after you. I never went back that night—I come on alone through the woods —but I never meant to give you trouble. I 'lowed to see her just once.—Now I'm done. This is the best way out of it.—Only say you'll be like you an' me was strangers!—Strangers" she repeated, and her voice broke from its hoarse whisper into a cry.

Bodewin shuddered. "Don't ask me that, Babe, for God's sake! That would be impossible. You don't see how useless it would be. — But, child, you are not going to die." He spoke wildly, with the horror upon him that she was dying already, and help so near. She did not speak. Her eyes were losing their expression — her breast heaved strangely, and one hand that lay on the ground moved like a wounded bird struggling in the leaves. Bodewin knew that he would give the promise. The cold sweat pricked out upon his forehead as he stooped, his lips close to Babe's ear.

"We will be strangers, Babe. No one shall ever hear of you from me — not if it costs me my good name," he groaned to himself.

Still she did not speak. — Still the fluttering hand and the long, struggling respirations. — He clasped her hand. "Babe, do you hear me?" The hand closed upon his and tightened with the hold of death upon life.

The miners off duty for the night who were lounging about the boarding-house steps, heard Bodewin's cry — as Josephine fancied she heard it, piercing the rumble of the car. They discussed the sound for a moment and then hurried down into the woods in the direction from which it came. It was a lifeless burden they carried up the hill. Bodewin walked behind it, wiping the blood from his cheek where a stone had cut him, making a slight wound. As they came out from the blackened wood, and the sky arched clear overhead, he looked up and saw Antares shining, a point of light, close to the moon's bright side. Bodewin did not yet know his fate.

Two hours afterwards Mr. Newbold sat on the piazza with a cigar which he was trying to smoke between his fingers. Josephine walked softly up and down; from time to time she looked at Bodewin, as he sat on the steps, his head between his hands. No one had spoken for many minutes. At last Josephine stopped behind her father's chair.

"Papa, do you think I may see — her — before they take her away?"

"If you ask what I think — I have told you already — it is no place for you."

"I should think it was any woman's place," said Josephine.

"There have been women enough, Lord knows. The room was full of them till the doctor turned them all out."

Mr. Newbold's temper always suffered when his sympathies were attacked. They had just been subjected to an unusual shock. The affair, besides, was a most unfortunate one for the mine. The Eagle Bird was notorious enough already, in all unprofitable ways.

"Will they take her down to the camp to-night, Bodewin?" he asked, raising his voice a little that it might penetrate Bodewin's abstracted mood.

"Yes," said Bodewin, without looking up.

"*How* will they take her, do you think?"

"The undertaker's wagon, I suppose."

"Papa," said Josephine, laying her hands softly upon his shoulders as she stood behind him, "why do you let them take her away? Why not let her friends find her here, among friends?"

"What are you talking about, Josephine?"

"I am asking you not to let that young girl be taken down to the camp, for everybody to look at. She was laid here at our door; let us take care of her."

"Don't be silly, Josephine. What do you call *our door?* What have we to do with it, except to regret it as a most shocking and unnecessary accident? I don't myself understand yet how it happened." Mr. Newbold cast an irritated glance towards the motionless figure on the steps. " Besides," he continued, jerking his chair forward a little on the painted floor, "she has not been identified. No one knows what sort of a story she may have attached to her. It looks very peculiar, to say the least."

Bodewin went down the steps and walked away towards the stables. He had got his old horse back again, with the scar on his hip from Tony Keesner's bullet. He went out to him, as to the only creature who could give him comfort that night. The faithful old comrade who asked no questions, who had never doubted or disowned his friend. He felt for the bony white nose in the darkness. Baldy recognized his master's step and his touch, though he had not spoken. He greeted him with sedate whinnyings, backing about in his stall to show his readiness for a night-ride if his master required it of him.

Josephine on the piazza was saying to her father: "Papa, do you remember the cabin in the woods I told you of, that Mr. Craig saw when he was lost, — and the wonderfully pretty girl? Is this girl beautiful?"

"Remarkably beautiful, I should say, for that class of girl."

"There cannot be so many such beautiful girls in a place like this."

"She may not belong to this place."

"Papa, I think I must see her. She might be the same one, you know."

"I should think Craig would be the best judge of that. He will see her to-morrow. However, there is nothing to prevent your seeing her, if you want to,—only don't ask me to go with you."

" Is any one with her? " asked Josephine.

" I believe there are some men waiting in the office. They have put her in the next room— Reed's bedroom. By George, if I were Reed, I shouldn't half like it."

Josephine went down to the door of the office and knocked. Two or three men within ceased talking as she entered. One of them rose and laid down his cigar. This was Mr. Reed, the assayer and engineer of the mine.

"I came to see the young girl who was killed," Josephine said hurriedly, feeling half ashamed of the intention, now she was about to carry it out.

" The body is in here, Miss Newbold,—please excuse the looks of the room," Mr. Reed said politely, as he opened the door. He was about to follow her in, when she hurriedly thanked him and begged to be allowed to go in alone.

It was a small room with a low board ceiling, painted white; the walls were merely wooden partitions, covered with hangings of a dark-red calico. Half of the room was occupied by the bed. A lamp on the floor behind it threw its shadow hugely over the wall and up on the ceiling above. In this shadow Josephine saw a motionless woman's form, partly covered by a shawl. The dust of the pass and the soot of the burnt forest were on her garments. Her travel-worn shoes were on her feet. As to her beauty there was no doubt. She lay on her back, at her fair length, her face turned a little aside showing the curve beneath the chin and the straightened line of neck behind the ear. The shadow of long lashes hid the sightless parting of the lids. Her long braids of hair, golden, with a silver light on it, were brought forward across her flattened shoulders, following the curve of her breasts and slipping out of sight between her arms and grandly sloping hips. There was all the tacit, slumbering pride of Babe's personality in her death-pose. A princess lying in state could not have mutely commanded more respect than this victim of ill-conditions at the climax of her life's defeat.

It was impossible not to feel that some remnant of consciousness must linger here to suffer from the intrusion of a stranger's pity. It gave. Josephine an almost hysterical sensation to think of the crowds that to-morrow would press around this form of sacred maidenhood, and stare at its beauty, and wonder at its history. Something that was not love nor pity, only a blind yearning of the human towards the human, across the impassable barrier, drew the living girl close to the dead. She laid her arms on each side of her, on the bed, her heart beating close above the one that was still, her breath warm on the white, half-averted face. She uttered no sound, but incoherent sobbing exclamations were struggling in her breast. The link between the lives of these two women, strangers to each other and subject alike to conditions others had made for them, was only made stronger by Babe's death.

Josephine stood awhile outside of the office door, looking out into the gray, melancholy moonlight. She saw Bodewin at a little distance, coming towards the house from the stables, walking unsteadily, with his head down. His unconscious figure seemed to bring upon her, all at once, a sense of all the unknown human misery that presses upon young lives and brings a sudden home-sickness in the midst of friends, and a pang of loneliness to the summer night. She burst into tears. Bodewin had seen her. He saw that she was weeping. He came to her quickly and took her hand in his. He knew where she had been.

"Don't cry so," he said. "There is so much trouble in this world that is worse than death."

"I know it — I feel as if there was trouble all around us to-night." She began to sob again.

"Not your trouble, I hope," he said, and then he murmured helplessly, "God bless you!" He lifted her hand and kissed it. The action startled her into stillness.

"Will you look at me?" he asked, still holding her by the hand. "Can you see my face?" — he turned it to the light.

"Yes," she said, trembling.

"Do I look like a man you could believe in, if his best friend deserted him, — if he were hunted for a villain?"

"Yes," said Josephine again.

His hand closed hard upon hers. "God bless you," he said again.

He walked beside her in silence to the steps of the porch, then he looked good-night or good-bye without speaking and left her. She saw him go back to the door of the office and sit down on the low step, in the moonlight.

"He does not know her," she said to herself; "yet, if he looks so when I am dead, I shall be satisfied."

She went to her room and lay upon her bed, in the white soft dress she had put on that evening because it was one of the dresses she had always been happy in, — and Bodewin had come home. She lay there, too miserable to light her lamp and undress herself; but at twelve o'clock the rattle of a wagon coming up the hill roused her. It stopped before the office door. Josephine sat up in bed, shuddering. She made the room light, drew her curtains close, and began hurriedly to take off her clothes. Her face was as pale as the sheets when she lay down in her bed again, leaving the lamp still burning.

She heard sounds below her window. Voices and footsteps of men, the grating of a heavy box pushed over the floor of the wagon, the click of the spring as the tail-board shut. The wagon drove away.

Bodewin walked behind it down the hill, and watched it out of sight along the dim, dusty, moonlit road to the camp.

CHAPTER XXI.

A MEETING IN THE WOOD.

CROWDS came and went the next day and looked at Babe, and no one spoke her name. No one came from the cabin in the wood. Mr. Craig had gone to Denver by the stage at four o'clock, before the Eagle Bird tragedy was generally known in the camp. There were two men who recognized her, but each, for his own reasons, kept the knowledge to himself. One was Harkins, who had arrived that morning by private team from the railroad terminus; the other was Hillbury. He had heard the particulars of the accident from Mr. Newbold.

" And Bodewin says he does not know her," he mused gloomily, when the story was finished.

"He does not say much of anything," Mr. Newbold replied, "but it is evident that he does not know her. It was a shocking thing for him. She was killed before his very face."

" Why did he follow her? "

"She was lurking around the house, as if she had some business she wanted to keep to herself. My daughter saw her first, crouching down among some boards close to the parlor windows. She pointed her out to Bodewin, who was on the piazza with her. The girl ran off when she found she was discovered, and Bodewin followed her, very naturally, I think. Haven't you seen Bodewin to-day?"

"No," said Hillbury.

"Well, I'm not surprised he don't want to talk about it. He is all 'broke up,' as they say out here. Harkins is in town, I hear. Came in his usual splendor. Pete Harrison's barouche and best team ordered by telegraph to meet him at the end of the track."

"Yes, I saw his arrival."

"I suppose he has come to look up his 'affidavit men,' as Sammis calls them, for the trial."

Hillbury gave Mr. Newbold a sudden look. He wondered if that amiably discursive gentleman could be aware that he had himself received, that morning, a summons to appear, under penalty of the law, as a witness for the Uinta against the Eagle Bird.

Colonel Harkins had arrived in the morning.

He had followed the stream of excitement to the undertaker's rooms and had looked at Babe, as Hillbury had looked at her, in silence. In the afternoon he ordered a horse saddled and rode away over the hills alone, to look at a "prospect" he had thought of buying for some Eastern parties, so he said. The way of his "prospect" was the way to the Keesner cabin, but before he came in sight of it he stopped and looked and listened intently, to make sure he was the only traveller in that part of the forest. While he was taking this precaution, he was aware of a horse's tread, muffled on the sodden pine-needles, but approaching distinctly from the direction of the pass. Harkins began whistling and looking about him at the trees, as if considering their value as timber. The horseman proved to be Tony Keesner, — Tony, more down-looking and sullen than usual, with a fierce spot of light in each of his narrow black eyes fixed on the distance.

"Tony is trailin' somebody," Harkins commented, quietly watching his approach.

Tony was in the mood to resent the unexpected appearance even of a friend. He transferred the gleam in his eyes from the indefinite distance to Harkins's face, without a change of expression.

"How are you, Anthony?" said Harkins, in a soft, grave voice. "How's the cabin, and how's all the folks?"

"Cabin's empty, all but Dad," Tony replied. _

"What have you done with the rest of the family?" Harkins asked.

Tony appeared to swallow something hard in his throat. It might have been rage — it could not have been tears. "They're clean gone; they lit out together las' night. I been huntin' 'em sence sun up; I been clear over the pass to Fairplay."

"You're off the scent, Tony. You're all off. I'm just from camp. Bodewin's there, sloshin' round as cool as quicksilver; and *Babe* is there. Tony, I've got some advice to give you and the old man, but I want to hear from you first. How did this thing happen? — You must 'a' been d—— careless."

They rode on slowly, side by side, towards the cabin, talking earnestly, Tony in quick, hard sentences, dropping like hailstones in the rain of Harkins's words. As they dismounted in front of the cabin and looked about them, each uttered in his own manner his favorite formula of profanity. The corral was empty, the cabin door was shut; the young setter dog howled and leaped against the door when he heard footsteps outside, but no voice from within bade him be quiet. A scrap of soiled white paper fluttered from the crack of the door, in which it had been wedged with a splinter of wood.

Harkins jerked out the wedge and handed the paper to Tony, with the question — "Is that the old man's fist?"

Tony acknowledged his father's handwriting. It addressed him briefly, as follows: —

"Tony I got word of her she aint livin I am goen down to Camp to clame the boddy."

Both men swore again, as if it were a kind of rite each felt bound to go through with, under the circumstances.

"How did he go? Has he got a horse?" Harkins asked sharply.

"Yes," said Tony, without moving his eyes from the paper in his hand. "He's took the black."

"Git after him, then, quick as you can! He couldn't have got word before noon. He's not to show himself in camp or to open his head till I'm ready for him. Understand? Tell him if he busts up my scheme again with his nonsense I'll see every mine he's got in ——, and himself, too, before I'll touch one of 'em. Look sharp now! You *sabe?*"

Harkins delivered these words in his low utterance, commanding Tony with his eyes as well as his voice. Harkins had eyes with a heavy fold of the lid projecting over them; ophidian eyes, with a sluggish power in them which better men than Tony Keesner had defied to their cost.

Tony hesitated — "You understand we've got to get even with Bodewin. It ain't waitin' and talkin' that'll do it," he said.

Harkins cursed him. "Haven't *I* got to get even with him? Do as I tell you, or by —— I'll have the sheriff after the old man and you too. You know who you're talkin' to!"

Tony knew. He put spurs to his horse and galloped away into the woods.

Mrs. Craig had asked Josephine to stay with her during Mr. Craig's absence, or until Miss Newbold herself left the camp with her father on their homeward journey, which was to include Denver and the trial. Josephine had gladly accepted the invitation for its own sake, and also because she wished to get away from the mine. The light comedy of Mrs. Craig's manner, her domestic confidences and foolish little household jokes, combined with her real sensitiveness and tact, were happily curative in their effect upon Josephine's excited nerves. She found herself laughing weakly, like a fever convalescent, on small occasion. It was a relief to talk about clothes, to put on her prettiest dresses for Mrs. Craig's benefit, and to experiment with her back hair at that lady's suggestions. She gave herself up to be petted and admired, as only a woman can pet and admire another woman who represents to her what her own youth has been or might have been. More than all was it a relief to hear Mrs. Craig talk about Bodewin in a frank, common-place way which took away something of the painful mystery Josephine's imagination had surrounded him with ever since his return. Mrs. Craig laughed at the idea of anything formidable connected with his reticence about his late adventure. "My dear, Bodewin is just like those little land 'turtles,' we used to call them when we were children. We used to catch them and knock on their shells and call to them to put out their heads; and, of course, they pulled them in as tight as they could squeeze. Depend upon it, your father and my husband, begging their pardons, have been knocking Bodewin on the shell and calling to him to put out his head. I know just how Joe and Bodewin are, together; they each bring out the other's most unpleasant traits. If *we* could have got Bodewin to ourselves when he first returned, I am perfectly certain we should know the whole story by this time. Bodewin isn't a man's man. I don't mean that he isn't a manly man. But he was born to be led by women — into trouble, and out of it. If only one woman could get him into permanent trouble by marrying him, and so keep him out of insane and promiscuous trouble, it would be a great relief to my mind. Bodewin isn't a bit of a genius that I know of, but I always feel for him that kind of unreasoning tenderness that geniuses and wilful, lovable children always inspire, — a predisposition which has no justice in it. I know that Bodewin's wife, if he had one, would have ever so much to forgive; but she would dote on his very faults."

"Perhaps if you had ever tried —" Josephine began, and stopped, coloring suddenly.

"— Being the wife of a genius?" laughed Mrs.

Craig. "Oh, my dear," she continued, with a slightly exaggerated gayety, "don't you know those little, reddish-blond men are *all* geniuses? Born to blush unseen, many of them, but that is an accident of fate." Mrs. Craig was talking recklessly, under the unwonted excitement of having another woman of surprising congeniality to listen to her. She would repent before she slept of half that she said to Josephine during the day, and then proceed to pile up more food for repentance the next day. Of two women who are intimate, as a rule, one talks and the other listens. Josephine listened and wondered a little, but was greatly amused and on the whole comforted and led away from her own unaccountable unhappiness.

Mrs. Craig was not so occupied with talking to Josephine that she did not see there was a change in her, since the early days of her visit to the camp. She was more interesting, more complicated. Has she had an experience, her hostess speculated; has she taken one of those sudden leaps of development girls of her age are subject to; or is it because she is away from home for the first time, in this exciting, consuming climate, among conditions altogether strange to her? Or is it because Bodewin never comes to ask her to ride in the valley?

Mrs. Craig was not so easy in her mind about Bodewin as she professed to be. And Hillbury, who had hitherto in her knowledge of him been the most sane and satisfactory of men, had developed an idiosyncrasy on his own account to match the general absurdity of things. He too, while hovering near them, avoided them as if under a vow.

The quarters of the government survey were not far from the Craig cabin. Mr. Hillbury was obliged to pass its door on his walks to and from the camp, unless he abandoned the ditch-walk for the woods. He thus found frequent occasion to bow to Josephine as she sat on the steps of the porch in the morning, the reflection from the sunny walk making her dark eyes luminous under the shade of her hat, or at evening, in the glow of sunset, her hands and arms bare to the elbows gleaming white in her lap. Sometimes he yielded to a reluctant fascination, and came across the foot-bridge for a few words with her, or even took a seat on the step below her, with the half-protesting air of one who owes it to himself to resist a pleasure within reach. But he never went in.

Mrs. Craig, amused and puzzled by his cautious attitude, teased him a little with playfully reiterated invitations; but Hillbury kept his outward defences secure against all her neighborly assaults and the more subtly undermining influence of Josephine's repose, — a repose unlike the bright directness of her manner as he recalled his first impressions of her. Hillbury would not have permitted himself to use the word in speaking of a girl like Josephine, but it was a repose charged with passion, as electricity slumbers in still, deeply colored evening skies. She talked little, but there was a divine intelligence in her face. Her movements were softer, she carried herself less unconsciously, her very hands had a different expression. Her eyes were less widely opened, and even when they rested upon indifferent things were full of an anxious tenderness. When they rested upon Hillbury he looked away and his blood behaved in a manner which would have interfered with the simplest scientific inquiry. Hillbury kept himself well under his own supervision, and these warnings did not escape his stern insight, but there were times when he rebelled against himself and asked himself why he had not an equal right with other men to make a fool of himself. Had he not already made a fool of himself about a man; why not then about a woman? The privilege of being inconsistent and probably unhappy was denied him by no one but himself. There were other stirrings and questionings in Hillbury's mind at this time. The unlaid ghost of his affection for Bodewin daily and nightly troubled his peace. On his way home along the ditch-walk one evening, close upon the eve of the trial, Hillbury's mind being full of that coming event, he was aware of a man standing on the foot-bridge opposite the Craig cabin, in an attitude that was painfully familiar. Hillbury approached more closely, and stopped when he had reached the bridge.

"Bodewin," he said, "may I have a few words with you?"

"Is that you, Hillbury? You know me then once more. That is kind of you."

Hillbury was not discouraged by the tone of Bodewin's words. "It is possible," he began, — and his fine accent and dispassionate manner at that moment were peculiarly irritating to Bodewin's morbid sensitiveness, — "that I may have done you some injustice in certain unhappy conclusions that have lately been forced upon me.

There is strong evidence against you. I have had to admit to myself that it is very strong. But I find I have an obstinate sentiment towards you, which does not rest on evidence. It is this sentiment which appeals to you now. I hope the appeal may not come too late. It should never be too late to acknowledge a wrong. Have I wronged you, Bodewin? You only can tell me if I have."

Hillbury waited for some sign from Bodewin. None came that could be interpreted as an answer to his appeal.

"Are you unwilling to confide in me? Do you consider the suffering you may be causing those who care for you, by a reticence that leaves such grave questions unanswered?"

"You say you have a sentiment still left for me which does not rest upon evidence?"

"I have. I have been suffering from it for many days."

"God prosper it, then, or else kill it quickly," said Bodewin, rather wildly. "I have no evidence to give you."

"You have nothing to say to me, then?"

"Are you my friend, did you say?"

"Are you an honest man?"

"Hillbury," said Bodewin, in his more natural manner, "I would that all men were as honest as I am, except these bonds."

"What bonds?"

"That I cannot tell you."

"There are bonds our sins make for us; there are other bonds which come from our duties. Are you in bondage to your body or your soul?"

"Do you expect me to answer your ghostly conundrums? Wait, and they will answer themselves," said Bodewin, with a return of his bitter flippance.

Hillbury looked at him sadly, trying in vain to read the expression of his face in the imperfect light, and then went on his way, past the cabin where Mrs. Craig and Josephine sat by the fire and talked of the coming trial.

"You must be *sure* to go!" Mrs. Craig was saying. "I'll never forgive you if you don't take the trouble to go and hear Joe's speech. It is a privilege his wife is debarred from because she is also the mother of his children; — and there is Bodewin's testimony. How *strange* it is that he hasn't been near us!" she exclaimed, suddenly forgetting her caution of many days.

Josephine's sigh echoed the word as she went

to the window and looked out. The water wim-
pled along darkly under the bridges and past the
lighted windows. Bodewin still hung over the
bridge rail where Hillbury had left him. His
bitterness against Hillbury was intensified by the
knowledge that to him in his calm deliberateness
were open all the opportunities he felt obliged to
deny himself, living, as he was, in the shadow of
vengeance. His bonds were heavy upon him. It
was incredible to him that Babe had not been
publicly recognized. It was incredible that her
father's or her brother's bullet had so long been
delayed. Bodewin knew the class of men they
belonged to. He knew their unappeasable pride
of vengeance; whether it would take the usual
form of a bullet delivered at sight or a shameful
story that would pursue him with a more deadly
aim, or both bullet and scandal, he could only
conjecture. In the meantime there was the trial,
with Mr. Craig as counsel for the Eagle Bird.

CHAPTER XXII.

THE case of the Uinta *versus* Eagle Bird was called in the afternoon. Mr. Newbold came back to his hotel to dinner that evening in high good humor. Harkins had made no fight at all, to speak of. He had rested his case on the records which Bodewin was ready to prove were not the true and original ones. His lawyer had talked through his nose and put his case before the jury in a slipshod way, on what he called its merits, without giving himself the trouble to make a speech. Thus said Mr. Newbold to Josephine, playing with her coffee-spoon, and dubious as to this easy victory. This was not the way, surely, by which Harkins had won his ill-omened reputation.

Josephine dressed herself to go into court with her father on the second day of the trial, with a nervous foreboding that it was to be one of the memorable days of her life. Her travelling dress, which she would have chosen to wear for its plainness, had received hard usage in the mountains. She put on instead the black satin with a dark shimmer of beads over the front, which she had worn the evening Bodewin had been presented to her. A little bonnet of gold-colored straw inclosed the crown of her head, and was tied under the chin with black velvet strings. She was buttoning her gloves, and getting very red in the cheeks while doing it, when a servant knocked with a note for her and a message from her father that he waited for her in the ladies' parlor.

"Tell him I am coming in a minute," she said, opening the note. "Oh, wait, please; is an answer wanted to this?"

"No answer, miss," the man replied, closing the door softly.

The note was written in a masculine hand Josephine did not remember ever to have seen before. She knew Bodewin's close, angular characters and Mr. Craig's legal scrawl. She had no other acquaintances in the town, that she knew of. The words of the note were : —

"If Miss Newbold would not miss a scene of peculiar interest to herself for other reasons than those connected with her father's pocket, she will not fail to be in the court-room to-day."

The note was not signed. Josephine tore it up with the sensation of having received an insult, and dropped the pieces into a tall china jar that stood by her toilet bureau. She took up a fan, somewhat too heavily perfumed, and began fanning herself absently. It was nine o'clock in the morning, but the sun was already hot in the street outside. The windows of her room were open, the blinds darkened, and the noise of continuous passing came in as she had often heard it at home, when they stayed in town after the summer heats began; only, instead of the heavy jar and rattle from the pavements, it was the more exciting rush of light wheels, and the pounding of hoofs on a hard, resonant road. Perhaps, she said to herself tremulously, it would be better she should not go into court that day; but could she miss this chance, perhaps the last one, of seeing Bodewin!

"What a color you have got!" her father said, looking at her as if taking, for the first time, a dispassionate view of her appearance.

"These hot strings always make my face flush."

Josephine put up her hand to the bow of her bonnet-strings, lifting her chin and letting her lashes fall.

"Why don't you wear something different?"

"This is the only bonnet I have here.

"Wear a hat then," Mr. Newbold suggested.

"A bonnet is the proper thing, papa. It is more conservative."

"If you want to be conservative, the thing to do is to stay at home."

"I promised Mrs. Craig I would hear her husband's speech," said Josephine, blushing at her own insincerity.

"Craig can't make a speech worth listening to! You will have to write her a lot of lies about it."

"Papa, I *wish* to go. I have always intended to go, since we first talked of the case. It cannot be so very unusual, or Mrs. Craig would not have asked me —"

"Come on then; but, by George —!" Mr. Newbold left his sentence unfinished, except by another look of rueful admiration at his daughter.

Mr. Craig in his opening speech gave a brief history of the dispute from the side of the defence, and said the defence would prove that the records by which the mine had been sold to Mr. Newbold were copies of the true and original ones; that the record of the original survey would be produced in evidence and sworn to by the man who made it.   He continued, that they could not prove the existing record on file to have been wilfully altered, but they could prove that the plaintiff had had an opportunity so to alter it, and they could also show the plaintiff to have been the author of a measure quite as arbitrary and illegal as the altering of loosely kept public records.   They could prove that he had caused a man, travelling peaceably on the public highway, to be seized and forcibly detained out of reach of his friends, or of communication with them, at a time when that man's liberty of action was inconvenient to the plaintiff.   Colonel Harkins at this point in his opponent's argument rose and left the court-room, returning with the Keesners, father and son, preceding him, with a noise of heavy boots, to seats near his own.   The elder Keesner was instantly recognized by a number of people in the court-room.   Mr. Craig had alluded to him in his speech as one of Harkins's "affidavit men," who had conveniently disappeared when the sale of the mine in his name had been accomplished.   His reappearance was regarded as a sign that Harkins had something in reserve for which the unexpected feebleness of his attack had been but a blind — an impression which made itself felt in an agreeable stir of revived interest.

Jim Keesner's long, wolfish visage looked haggard in the strong light, among faces which showed better conditions. Tony's face was not generally known, but it excited attention for its sullen, picturesque beauty. As he took his seat, his head came between Josephine and her view of Bodewin, sitting at a distance, across the room. She had only ventured to look once at Bodewin, and had not been able to guess from the expression of his lowered eyes and pale set profile what his frame of mind might be.

The Keesners had entered the court-room with that exaggerated sense of isolation under observation which persons unused to a large assemblage of people are apt to have, appearing in one under circumstances momentous to themselves. Tony kept his eyes down, under an impression that everybody in the room was looking at him. When at length he raised them, with a forced air of defiant indifference, he met Josephine's eyes fixed upon him in wondering, startled recognition.

The expression of her face meant nothing to him. He only felt its beauty, with a shock of

his savage blood as he had felt it for the first
time on the rocks in the blinding sunlight of
Mike's claim. He hated her for making him
feel the distance between them. He hated Bodewin for being the man who had sat at her side
on the rocks and talked to her with a fulness
and ease of expression which might be supposed
to please women but could only excite the contempt of men.

Josephine was no longer looking at or apparently conscious of him. Since it was out of his
power to produce any other kind of impression
upon her, he fell into visions of how he might
hurt her with brute force. How he might press
the color out of her cheeks with his two hard
hands and see it rushing back again with helpless
tears to the proud dark eyes. He could see the
shape of her arms defined by her close-fitting
dress, as she sat opening and shutting her fan.
He shuddered slightly and set his teeth, imagining
himself crushing their firm roundness in his grip.

Mr. Craig was closing his speech. "Gentlemen," he was saying to the jury, "what we are
obliged to do is to consider the character of the
plaintiff in the light of this most characteristic
deed. Bear in mind, it was not done as to John

Bodewin, but as to any man whom the plaintiff wished temporarily to get out of his way. Had he desired to get him out of his way permanently, doubtless means would have been found to accomplish it. If either you or I, gentlemen, should, in the peaceful conduct of our affairs, be so unfortunate as to get in the plaintiff's way, we might expect to be disposed of as summarily as our witness was disposed of. The plaintiff is well known, wherever speculation in mines is carried on, as a man whom it is not only useless but dangerous to balk in the accomplishment of his schemes. Why? Because he has no scruples that interfere with his pursuit of other men's property. He belongs to the predatory class of men. He has no responsibilities as to his future, or regrets as to his past. He glories in his successful crimes. He boasts of the power he claims to have of bending even the law to his purposes. Are we preparing for him another triumph of this kind? We are Western men; we want to encourage Eastern capitalists to seek investments in the West. One way to do it will be to show them that their investments *in* the West can and will be protected *by* the West. The misfortune of one Eastern property-owner will be a warning to a hundred others. It is just such men as the plaintiff in this suit — and not many like him would be needed to do it — who ruin the business of legitimate mining in the West."

Another ill-omened pair of eyes had dwelt upon Josephine's face during a greater portion of the time Mr. Craig was speaking. Colonel Harkins considered himself a judge of female beauty, and decided on deliberate inspection that Josephine's charms had not been overstated by rumor. He was looking at her when Mr. Craig unexpectedly brought forth the words, " Bear in mind, it was not done as to John Bodewin." The Colonel was not a sensitive observer, but he could not fail to see that Josephine's face turned scarlet, as if her own name had been suddenly called in court in an oratorical tone of voice. He saw that she kept her eyes upon the speaker's face with a slight knitting of the brows, while the flush in her cheeks subsided, revived again, and faded into a marked paleness. " *She* is tender in that quarter, too. — What the devil ails the women, to take after a cold-blooded sneak who can't tell which girl he wants till he has lost them both!" The Colonel's large, light felt hat reposed on the angle of his crossed knees. A crimson rosebud rested against the silk lining of his coat-lapel. His jaws projected squarely on either side of his Napoleon III. mustache and imperial, grizzled like the short, stiff hair on his massive head. He nursed an unlit cigar between his lips, and occasionally changed it from one corner of his mouth to the other, or tipped it sarcastically upwards towards the blunt beak of his nose. He listened with perfect equanimity to Mr. Craig's theory of his character and exposition of his methods; this was, in fact, one of Harkins's great days.

Sammis, looking· brilliantly sunburned, in a new suit of clothes, was the first witness for the defence. He testified to the burning of the Gem Saloon, where the records of the camp had been kept in the days of its infancy. To the fact that Harkins had the records in his undisturbed possession for a day and a night, and part of the following day. That the proprietor of the Gem Saloon was known to have no insurance on his property and no ready money. That, in spite of having lost everything, he was notoriously better off after the fire than before it. Sammis bore his cross-examination well; but a friend of his who remembered some suspicious circumstances connected with the fire, found, under the opposite lawyer's questioning, that he had remembered too much.   Another gentleman, who testified as to the position of the boundary monuments and declared that they had been changed within the time of his residence in the camp, was brought to the verge of tears by the unsympathetic manner of the plaintiff's counsel and the confusion in his own dates.   But this gentleman had escaped Mr. Craig's supervision during the morning hours and had stimulated his memory with unwise potations.

Bodewin took his place on the witness-stand in a general silence of expectation.   The real contest was now understood to have begun.

He testified that he had surveyed the Uinta and Eagle Bird claims in the spring of 1877. That he had believed Harkins to be the owner of both claims at that time, although the record of survey for the Eagle Bird was made out in the name of James Keesner.

The records of both surveys, preserved in Bodewin's note-book, were produced and sworn to by him and examined by the jury.

Bodewin was shown a copy of the present record, and swore that it was not a true representation of the two claims.   He explained the points of difference, and the new record was also given to the jury to compare with the original one.

One of the jurymen asked how a change could be made in a record on paper without its being evident on examination. Bodewin replied that a new record could be substituted, giving an entirely different description of the same property, the records of the camp at that time not having been bound together, but kept loosely, each one folded separately, in a candle-box, as a former witness had testified.

Here Mr. Craig made a pause, during which the witness appeared to be slightly restless.

"Mr. Bodewin," the counsel for the defence began again, "you started to cross the range on horseback on the morning of the 5th of September?"

After a moment's hesitation, as if considering the date, Bodewin answered: "Yes."

"Was it your intention in starting on that ride to appear as a witness on this case, then called for the 6th?"

"It was."

"Why did you not fulfil that intention?"

"I was prevented from doing so."

"State the nature of the impediment, if you please."

" It was of the nature of two men, armed with pistols and rifles."

" With these weapons pointed at you ? "

" The pistols, yes."

" And by these means they induced you to change the course of your journey ? "

" They did."

" The inducement was sufficient, I presume ? "

Mr. Craig had asked his questions in quick succession, in his nervous manner; Bodewin replying in a much lower voice, with a curious, defensive expression in his heavy-lidded eyes, raised not quite to the level of Mr. Craig's.

" Were these men known to you ? "

" They were not."

" Had you ever seen them before?"

" I had seen one of them once before, without knowing his name."

" State where on the road between here and the camp you met with this impediment."

" It was not on the direct road between here and the camp."

" Where was it ? "

"It was on the trail which joins that road on the other side of the pass."

"You were then on your way to the pass?"

"No." Bodewin could not resist a pause during which he enjoyed Mr. Craig's ill-concealed discomfiture, and then added calmly: "I had nearly reached the foot of the pass when I was overtaken by one of these men, who induced me to return with him to a spot in the timber where, he said, a man lay wounded by the falling of his horse, who had an important message for me which he would only deliver in person. I went back with the supposed messenger's messenger, by the way of this trail, found a man lying on the ground, apparently helpless and in pain; I dismounted to receive his message and was then easily made prisoner."

Bodewin was answering with reckless promptness, so far as the condition of his promise would permit. If Mr. Craig, in the insanity of his zeal, insisted upon putting questions his witness could not or would not answer, he must take the consequences.

"What was the nature of that message they trapped you with, Mr. Bodewin?"

"It was of a personal nature."

Mr. Craig did not press the question, though

inwardly raging at Bodewin's impertinence, and longing for an opportunity to punish it.

"Were you forcibly prevented from returning to your home and occupation during all the time you were absent?"

"That may be a matter of opinion."

"How do you mean?"

"I was constantly kept in sight by one or both of my keepers, they carrying weapons, while I was unarmed. They informed me that if I kept quiet I would not get hurt, the inference being that if I did not keep quiet, I would."

"Under these circumstances you naturally kept pretty quiet."

Bodewin did not smile at or reply to this pleasantry.

"Was Colonel Harkins's name mentioned at any time between you and your captors during the time of your confinement?"

"It was."

"Give the conversation or conversations as nearly as you can recall them relating to Colonel Harkins."

"I remember but one conversation in which his name was mentioned. I cannot repeat it word for word."

"What impression did it leave on your mind as to Harkins's connection with your capture and imprisonment?"

"I have not said that I was imprisoned —"

"Your restraint, then."

"It left the impression that Colonel Harkins was solely responsible for both."

"Where did they run you off to?" one of the jurymen asked.

Mr. Craig interposed, saying that his witness did not wish to criminate those persons who had carried into execution the plan of his abduction, regarding them, with characteristic magnanimity, as tools merely, in the hands of a power much more dangerous than themselves.

"There is a humane breadth of view," Mr. Craig continued, permitting himself an attempt at sarcasm, which he fancied would escape everybody but the object of it, "a humane breadth of view which but few of us can boast of, which enables us to sympathize even with those who have tried to injure us, when we understand and pity their circumstances. We look upon them as injured themselves, in proportion as they are injuring us, by their enslavement to an evil influence —"

"Oh, that's all nonsense!" said the lively juryman. "Tell us where they hid you!"

The court protected Bodewin in refusing to answer the question, perhaps because it interfered with the court's dignity for jurors to assist at the examination of witnesses; but an unfavorable opinion was inevitably formed of the witness, as a person of high moral pretentions and unaccountable reserves, whose own actions would require close watching.

This opinion prevailed thenceforward among the men who were present, but the women generally respected Bodewin for keeping his own secrets and protecting his enemies. They were predisposed towards him for other reasons, that would not sound so well in statement. They liked his youthful slenderness of person, the easy way in which he wore his well-cut clothes. They observed, those who were nearest to him, that his hands, although nearly as brown as an Indian's, were long, smooth, and refined-looking. They liked his Eastern accent, his quiet answers, and the slumbering intensity of expression, impossible to define, in his heavy-lidded, grayish eyes. They hoped he would come off well on the cross-examination.

The court now took a recess.

CHAPTER XXIII.

THE REBUTTAL.

THE afternoon sitting opened cheerfully with Bodewin's cross-examination. The men with few exceptions had lunched, and with vests opened on account of the increasing heat, were prepared to enjoy the baiting of this probably conceited young man, who took such airs of gloomy reticence and whose information seemed to be so largely in excess of his desire to impart it.

The lawyer for the plaintiff, listening with apparent negligence to Bodewin's account of his capture, saw that it was a tale calling for but little talent in the cross-examination to make ridiculous to a Western jury. It had excited marked surprise in the court-room among those present who knew Bodewin by reputation as a cool fellow and a man of long experience in the West, well acquainted with the risk of solitary journeys in that part of the country, at a time

when scarcely a week passed without a stage
being stopped and a file of passengers called on
to "hold up their hands." The weakness of
Bodewin's story was brought out and embellished
with local allusions and such wit as the speaker
had at his command. He enlarged upon Bodewin's
magnanimity, as Mr. Craig had called it, towards
his captors. Such magnanimity was certainly
unusual, and to a stranger, unacquainted with
the character of the witness, seemed to demand
some further explanation, besides that transcen-
dent Christian forbearance which the learned
counsel on the other side had attributed to his
witness.

Was the witness quite sure that he had not
some other and more natural, not to say human
reason for condoning such a serious and exasper-
ating offence as the restraint of his person and
actions, at a time when both were imperatively
required elsewhere? Had captivity by chance
been sweetened to him? We are commanded
to love our enemies, but no law, civil or religious,
that the counsel could remember, required a man
to keep his enemies' secrets; especially when
they were secrets of a nature likely to be damag-
ing to his own character. There were usually two

sides to bargains of that kind. "Now, as to that message," the plaintiff's counsel asked suddenly, in the hardest of his nasal tones, "might one ask, since it was of so personal a nature, if it was a message from a lady?" There was said to be a lady in every case; the lawyer hoped this case was not to be an ungallant exception to the rule. Bodewin was again supported by the court in his refusal to answer, but the lawyer's wit was of the kind which makes the average juryman grateful to its author. The weightier but less amusing portions of Bodewin's testimony were lost sight of in the story of his capture, which could ill bear the scrutiny Harkins's counsel had succeeded in concentrating upon it, while calling upon the jury to wonder at the witness's reasons for twice refusing to answer the questions put to him. The juror who had been snubbed by the court was in no doubt whatever as to the duplicity of Bodewin's character, and the general feeling was against him, when Mr. Craig said, at the close of his examination : —

"Your Honor, this rests the case for the defence."

A mingled stir of relief and expectation had begun to pervade the court-room, when the plain-

tiff's counsel rose and said that he would like to
introduce a few witnesses in rebuttal. People
who were leaving the room returned to their
seats again, and no one was surprised when the
name of James Keesner was called. They would
now have the story of the surveys and sale of
the Eagle Bird over again from Harkins's side.

James Keesner testified that on the 5th of
September, somewhere about noon, John Bodewin
came to his cabin in the north woods near the
lake, and asked him to let him stay there quietly
until the Eagle Bird trial was over. That he had
known Bodewin, off and on, for some years,
through Colonel Harkins; that Colonel Harkins
had said, Bodewin would never testify against
him on account of something that passed between
them at Deadwood three years ago, something
about a woman, that Bodewin didn't want talked
about. That Bodewin didn't explain to them
why he did not wish to go on the trial, but just
said he didn't want to and wouldn't, and wanted
to stay there till the trial was over. That Bodewin had been to the cabin before, not often, but
once or twice that summer as he was passing
through the woods. The cabin had been built
three years before, when they were working the

claim near it; they had quit work on the claim for a year, and had only been back there since spring. That they lived very quiet in the woods, Bodewin keeping close to the cabin on account of not wanting to be seen by any one passing. That he and the witness's daughter Louisa, called Babe, were always together, he helping her about her work or just sitting around looking at her. That Babe was seventeen and worth looking at. She wasn't used to men like Bodewin, that called themselves gentlemen. That a year or so before, Bodewin had sent her his picture in joke like, by Harkins, hearing Harkins say what a beauty she was growing. That he set himself to make her like him. That it was easy done. That he, the witness, had been troubled about the way things looked, but thought it best not to say anything, Bodewin being there for so short a time and Babe as innocent as the day she was born. That he was watching out for them, the evening before they went off. Bodewin was sitting on the bench in front of the cabin, talking low with Babe, their heads close together, that he himself kept walking up and down, up and down, pulling on his old pipe, and watching out behind the trees; that when he could not see them any longer for night coming on, he came up short to them and ordered them into the house. Bodewin had looked mad and gone straight to bed. Babe was for going off too, but he had kept her by and given her a talking to.

Perhaps he had been hard on her, but what was a man to do with such foolishness going on, and Babe his only girl and her mother dead. He described the situation of the rooms in the cabin and went on with his story. How in the morning, early, Tony had gone out for water and found the black horse was missing and they two the only ones left in the cabin. Bodewin was gone, and Babe was gone. Her bed had not been slept in. The boards of the floor had been taken up to make room for Bodewin to crawl up from below. If his girl had gone wrong, it was the fault of Bodewin's ways, different to what she was used to, and his being continually round trying to make her like him, and she having no mother or woman to talk to her. Any one who ever saw his girl could see she was a good girl. She hadn't had any chance, anyhow, to be anything else.

Here Keesner paused and wiped his face and beard. His lean hands were trembling, and his voice was hoarse with the excitement of speech in the presence of so large and attentive an audience. Under his unfeigned trouble, there was the satisfaction of being himself a figure of unwonted importance on an occasion likely to be memorable in that region.

"Did I ever see my girl again?" he repeated. "Never, either living or dead,—but plenty saw her. There isn't a man from the camp in this room, I may say, but has seen her, and can speak to what I say, that she was well-grown and handsome, with as good a look to her as any girl need to have. Nobody that ever saw her could take her for any poor truck. She was born a long ways from any of your camps or cities, either. She knew the look of the trees better than she did men's looks. She was easy lied to."

Being recalled to his narrative, Keesner went on to say that Tony, his son, wouldn't eat nor sleep, but was hunting Bodewin, while he himself stayed by, in case Babe should come home. That in the afternoon the black horse came straying back through the woods, the saddle on but the stirrups crossed over the saddle and the bridle hanging from the pommel. That the next afternoon, being the day but one after Babe left,

Harkins rode out to the cabin and told him his girl was dead — dead, but first deserted by the man that led her away.

"This day week," said Keesner, "my girl was buried by strangers. She was stoned to death by the emptying of a car while she was crossing the waste-dump up at the Eagle Bird, where she'd come a-huntin' for John Bodewin. Gentlemen," said the witness, turning his red, convulsed countenance upon the jury, "that man Bodewin walked behind my girl's dead body when they carried her up the hill to the mine; he heard all the fuss and the racket, and he never said a word. He saw her layin' there for the whole town to stare at — with the very shoes on her feet she'd followed him in away from her home, and he never said a word; never owned to it he'd ever set eyes on her before — never once said she was a good girl, with folks of her own belonging to her. He let them say what they would of her. She was nothin' to him no more."

"Why didn't Colonel Harkins say he knew her?" Keesner repeated in answer to the counsel's question. "Because when he see my daughter layin' there, and nobody to claim her, he knew it meant trouble, the kind of trouble that's better not talked of. He knowed Babe never got in that shape without help. 'Who's the man?' he says to me. 'John Bodewin's the man,' I says. 'You want to git even with him?' he says. 'That's what I'm layin' for,' says I. 'Hold on, then. Wait,' says he, 'your time'll come. Words bite sharper than bullets when a man's thin-skinned.' And I've hel' on and I've waited, and now I've said my say, and you can ask Anthony, my son there, if every word ain't God's truth."

Mr. Craig sat stupefied, making no effort to impede the witness or arrest his words by timely objections. The case had gone out of his hands and beyond him. It was no longer a question of Mr. Newbold's property, but of John Bodewin's honor. The lady who sat next to Josephine was weeping hysterically. Men were muttering together. Mr. Craig, fearing that Keesner's story might only gain strength on investigation, and seeing that the witness had the whole court with him, waived his right of cross-questioning, and the next witness was called.

In the conference before the trial, between Harkins and the Keesners, in the cabin in the wood, Tony had stipulated that "Dad" should "do the lyin'." He "was used to it"—as for himself, the less talking they made him do the better. Harkins had accepted Tony's estimate of his own powers, and he was not called upon to corroborate the more fanciful portions of his father's narrative. But the parts which Harkins had supplied, assuring his confederates that they were necessary to complete Bodewin's disgrace, were not the strongest parts of James Keesner's story. There remained enough which Tony could savagely confirm without fear of entanglement.

There was only one more witness for the rebuttal. The friendship between Bodewin and Hillbury was not generally known to the excited group of people who awaited the next development in this singular trial; but to one or two of those whose suspense was keenest, the painfulness of the scene reached its climax when the name of Edward Wales Hillbury was called by the counsel for the plaintiff.

Mr. Craig was sharply roused by it. His old dislike for Bodewin, lately intensified by their mutual relations, had never been inconsistent with respect. He looked at Bodewin keenly, and said to himself, "Here has been some cruel lying. Hillbury will be sorry for what he is going to do, if he could have helped doing it. I'll make him sorry for it!" the perverse little lawyer vowed to himself. Now that there seemed to be abundant cause for distrusting Bodewin, he suddenly felt himself bound to do battle for him. Besides, Bodewin was his witness.

Hillbury's direct examination brought out the fact of his accidental visit to the cabin in the woods and his interview with Babe, including the incident of Bodewin's photograph. Babe had informed her father of this visit in detail, knowing him to be engaged in a plot of some kind against the original of the picture, and hoping that it might frighten, or possibly deter him through fear of discovery. Keesner had treasured up his daughter's communication as likely to be interesting to Harkins. Harkins had found it extremely interesting, and the result of Babe's warning had been Hillbury's summons to testify against his friend.

The counsel then asked Hillbury if Mr. Bodewin had ever said anything to him which would lead him to suppose that Colonel Harkins had any hold upon him. Hillbury replied with evident reluctance that Mr. Bodewin had once said that he was under an obligation to Colonel Harkins. Repeated questions forced from him the admission that Mr. Bodewin had spoken of the obligation as a delicate and strenuous one, but added that Mr. Bodewin often used extravagant expressions in speaking of quite simple matters, and declared that he had attached no particular importance to the words.

"At the time," the counsel suggested.

"At the time," Hillbury allowed the suggestion.

"At any subsequent time did you regard them more seriously?"

"When Mr. Bodewin was suddenly missing, I naturally recalled everything, even the slightest noteworthy thing, connected with him that had happened near the time of his disappearance, this conversation among others."

Hillbury then identified the unknown girl who was killed at the Eagle Bird mine as the one he had seen and talked with in the cabin. When asked if Mr. Bodewin had ever spoken to him of this girl or of the cabin, the witness replied that he had not.

"You were then greatly surprised to find his photograph there, were you not?" the counsel asked.

"I was."

"Did you ever question him about it?"

"I did not."

"Why not?"

"For one reason, there was no opportunity to do so, between the time of my visit to the cabin and Mr. Bodewin's disappearance."

"You have had opportunities since his return to speak to him about it, have you not?"

"I have."

"Still you made no allusion to this incident which was such a matter of surprise to you?"

"No, not directly?"

"Have you ever in any way invited his confidence on this subject?"

"In a general way I have invited his confidence on this and other subjects."

"Did he respond?"

"He did not. But, it may be that my manner was at fault. One is not always happy on such occasions; and it has never been my habit to press inquiries of a personal nature upon my friends."

"And you wish I would be equally considerate with you—" the counsel concluded with a flourish of courtesy. "That will do, Mr. Hill-bury."

Mr. Craig began his cross-examination by

asking Hillbury how long he had known Mr. Bodewin.

"Fifteen years," was the reply.

"Had their relations during that time been friendly?"

"Yes."

"Invariably?"

"Yes."

What were their relations at the present time? Hillbury's momentary hesitation was covered by an objection promptly raised by the opposite counsel. The question was allowed, and Hillbury replied that he was not in a position to say how Mr. Bodewin might regard him at that moment, but the answer had the effect of an evasion, and Mr. Craig felt that he had gained his first point. How was it, he next asked, that a friend of Mr. Bodewin's, one who had been his friend for fifteen years, had made no search for him, when he was missing under circumstances calculated to excite the gravest apprehensions for his safety?

Mr. Hillbury replied that the organized search set on foot by the town stood a better chance of success, in cases of that kind, than would a single individual, even with the stimulus of his friendship for the object of the search.

"The organized search," Mr. Craig retorted, "consisted of three or four men who rode about the country, and drank a little more whiskey than usual for a few days; the search then resolved itself into gossip about Bodewin's character and intentions, and bets as to his probable fate. Was that enough to satisfy a friendship of fifteen years?"

"I did not say that it was," Mr. Hillbury replied.

"Well, was it?"

"In my own case, it was not."

"What further effort, if any, did you make to find your friend?"

"I went in search of him myself."

"Oh, indeed! And how much time, pray, did you give to this individual search?" asked Mr. Craig, who knew that Hillbury had been seen in camp or its neighborhood nearly every day during Bodewin's absence.

"A little more than half a day."

"I suppose you found him," Mr. Craig said, with an ironical glance at the jury.

Mr. Hillbury made no response to this supposition.

"Were you satisfied with the result of your half-a-day's search?"

"In one sense, yes."

"In what sense was that?"

"In the sense that I found him."

A sensation in the court, in the midst of which Mr. Craig's irony was extinguished.

"Where did you find him?" he asked mechanically, while desperately trying to arrange his future questions, in case Hillbury's answer should turn out to be as bad as he feared.

"In the cabin in the North woods."

"Which cabin?"

"The one I have already described where I saw the photograph of Mr. Bodewin."

"What was Mr. Bodewin doing when you found him, as you say?" Mr. Craig was now trusting to the chance of getting the witness involved by rapidly multiplying unimportant questions. Hillbury's pale countenance facing him began to show signs of distress. Mr. Craig pressed the question.

"What was he doing?"

"I don't know *what* he was doing," said Hillbury, with a kind of violence.

"How near were you to him?"

"Twice as far from him, perhaps, as I am from you."

"Yet you don't know what he was doing! Did you ask him?"

"I did not speak to him."

"You did not speak to him! What did you do, pray?"

"I looked at him, and then went back to my horse, mounted and rode away."

"A singular and touching interview, truly, between friends of fifteen years, one of whom had been missing for some time under an implication of danger. Was Mr. Bodewin alone when you saw him and were too much overcome, as I conclude, by your feelings, to speak to him?"

"He was not."

"Who was with him?"

"A young woman."

"Any one else?"

"To all appearances they were alone."

"Were they talking together?"

"No."

"Well, 'to all appearances' what were they doing?" Mr. Craig went on stupidly; but a strange look in Hillbury's face, almost like a warning unspoken, arrested him. "Did Mr. Bodewin see you, or know of your neighborhood?" he hurried on, trying to bury the previous question in a new one.

"I do not think he did," said Hillbury, dropping his eyes. He knew that Craig had understood him at last, and that the ordeal was over.

But Craig could not accept his defeat without one more effort.

"You were there, then, not to find your friend but to spy upon his actions?"

"I was there to find him, to help him if he needed such help as I alone could give him, to procure additional help if required. Finding him safe and apparently happy, I did not offer my services. The offer of my society it seemed better, under the circumstances, to postpone."

"Have you ever described this incident before?"

"I have never spoken of it until to-day."

"You seem to have saved it carefully for the time when it would be most likely to injure your friend of fifteen years."

"That is your inference, for which I am not responsible."

Hillbury was released, inwardly cursing Craig

for a "rash, intruding fool," and writhing under his own revolting part in the day's work. And Craig could think of nothing that would have made things worse, except to have had his wife present to witness his blunders.

CHAPTER XXIV.

THE NIGHT AFTER THE TRIAL.

IT was the talk of the town that evening that Harkins had won his suit, Bodewin, the chief witness for the defence, having forsworn himself, and his testimony having been practically set aside by the jury. That there had been shameful disclosures as to his character. That Tony Keesner, brother of the girl he had wronged, was hunting for Bodewin, swearing he would shoot him at sight. Bets were being offered in every drinking-saloon of the city as to the result of the meeting. The town seemed to have emptied itself into the streets, at this hour of coolness and gayety. Children's voices were shrill in the gardened suburbs; the light rush of wheels was loud and low, in quick alternation, on the broad avenues looking outward from the city. A wind from the mountains, setting across the sun-warmed plain, revived with its wild, sweet breath the day's languors.

How many heart-breaks go to make up that song of a city at night! On her bed, that loomed white in the darkened room, Josephine lay and listened to this voice of many voices, dream-like, far away from that burning core of anguish which was the centre of her being. Shame could not approach Bodewin as he lived in her thoughts. He had loved the girl who was dead, there had been a necessity for secrecy, everything had been misjudged and misrepresented, and Bodewin had been too proud or too wretched to explain. That he had been base it was out of the power of the woman who loved him to believe. That he loved the girl whose beauty still ached in Josephine's remembrance, she could well believe. That her death had complicated his position in some cruel way, she could understand — or rather she tried to understand nothing; she believed and suffered. But the dumb cry of her anguish was not for her-self — it was for Bodewin. Where was he that night? What had been left to him? Everything was gone, and there lived not a soul who could comfort him. She had dreamed that they two were strangely, perhaps perilously, sympathetic, but while she had been balancing her maidenly subtleties of conduct, the current of his life had sunk out of sight, like those rivers that run along in sunshine and then suddenly disappear in the quicksands.

About nine o'clock that evening, in one of the thoroughfares of the town, two pistol-shots were heard, fired in quick succession. Word was borne from street to street, with a clamor of voices and a hurry of feet, that Harkins in the hour of his triumph was dead. It reached the great, gaslit house, with its tiers of balconied windows, open to the night, where Josephine lay; it floated up from smoking-room to parlor, and pervaded the corridors in bursts of excited talk. It reached Josephine's door in a sound of imperative knocking. She started up. Her father spoke to her from the passage. She rose and opened the door. The room was faintly lighted from the street.

"Sitting in the dark, Jose?" her father said, reaching for her hand. "I hoped you were in bed and asleep, but I came up, thinking you might have been wakened by the stir in the house. A dreadful thing has happened. The town is ringing with it! Did you hear the shots?"

Josephine did not answer.

Her father had drawn her down upon his lap,

in the great chair he had sunk into. He sighed, and rubbed his handkerchief over his damp forehead.

"That last shot sent Harkins to his account!"

"Who —" Josephine began, and the great dread in her eyes finished the question.

"He and that young Keesner were in some place drinking together, or Keesner was drinking and Harkins was keeping watch of him. Keesner saw Bodewin pass on the street. He rushed out and fired one shot at him, and missed. Harkins followed him and grabbed him from behind, before he could shoot again. Keesner whirled, and in the struggle Harkins got the second barrel. They fell together, Harkins underneath. He never spoke. Keesner's friends got him away before the police came up. But Harkins got what was meant for Bodewin. Why, Josephine!"

Josephine was sobbing on her father's neck. "Thank God!" she whispered, not knowing that she had spoken.

Bodewin had brought his horse down from the mountains, intending to leave him on a ranch for the winter. He had himself expected to go East after the trial; but now he had no plans, only to get out of the town as quickly as possible, and alone. Across the plains many roads and trails led towards the distant mountain passes, to the South and West.

Baldy had found a trail and was following it, with his head low, his ears playing backwards and forwards, knowing that his master had given him the direction of their course, and intelligently responsive to the trust.

Where he was going, what he was going to do, Bodewin did not yet know. It was enough for the present that he was in motion. But the motion was not so rapid or so exciting as to take the place of thought. The darkness was peopled with faces, poignant with wounded surprise or reproach or contempt, their looks all concentrated upon himself as in a nightmare. Babe Keesner's face he saw more constantly and vividly than any other. Although he could not definitely accuse himself, his conscience was not clear when he thought of her. Of all who had suffered through him, she had suffered most, and she had lost everything. Now that it was too late he could see the madness of his course with regard to her — the blind pertinacity with which he had kept that wild and foolish promise her

death had extorted from him. From the night
when he followed the wagon that bore her body
to the camp, he had felt that he was marked for
trouble; but he had not foreseen that it could
involve any one but himself. He might have
asked for another hearing at the trial, for Babe's
sake if not for his own, but he could not have
gone on the witness stand again without being
summoned and questioned by Craig — Craig who
could not know what questions to ask, and
whose capacity for blundering might be measured
by his cross-examination of Hillbury. He would
not have been allowed to tell an uninterrupted
story without a running fire of objections from the
opposite counsel. He had no proofs to offer that
easy and cynical crowd to which his appeal must
have been made, except his own word, and that
had been broken down before them. These were
some of the excuses which Bodewin made for a
silence which covered so much wrong and pain;
but the true explanation of it lay deeper than all
his reasons, in the nature of the man himself.
No one who knew him well would have been
surprised that he was silent — after hearing his
reputation sworn away before an assemblage of
men ready, to a man, to believe him guilty, even

had he felt that there was a single person present to whom his disgrace mattered more than to Hill-bury — Hillbury, whose testimony had completed the case against him.

Bodewin's anguish, when he thought of Josephine, left no room for conjecture as to what she might have felt in witnessing his shame. The trial scene had branded him for life. The infamy of it was known to but a few people, but it would spread. Already he could hear the story of it repeated in every city where he had ever been known. There was nothing to be done but to live it down in the years that were left to him of his life. He felt already old, and yet as if he should never die. In the meantime he would do Babe the justice and give himself the consolation of telling the true story to Josephine. That she would believe him, without proofs, he did not doubt. Such generous belief was one of the necessities of her nature. He would get away into some corner of the world where he was not known, and think it all over and write her a letter. Already there was a strange, poor comfort in the thought.

CHAPTER XXV.

JOSEPHINE AND HILLBURY.

JOSEPHINE had been home nearly a month when Bodewin's letter came. It was a thick letter with the postmark only of some railroad. on the envelope. She opened it, with the joyless certainty that she was to read the story of Babe Keesner written by her unhappy lover. There were a number of sheets closely written without date or signature, and within them was a note addressed to herself. She read: —

"MY DEAR MISS NEWBOLD: When I asked you on the night of Babe Keesner's death if you could still have faith in me, even if circumstances condemned me, I spoke in weakness, foreseeing what some of the consequences of that night were likely to be, and feeling that the one thing I could not bear was that you should doubt me. It is a consolation to me, even now, to remember how readily and cordially you replied to my presumptuous claim upon your faith. You were in distress yourself that night. I frightened and bewildered you, yet I remember you did not shrink from me or evade my selfish question. You must have thought of it in the court-room, and it must have seemed to you a shameless and paltry advantage for me to have taken of your generosity. I dare not picture to myself all that you must have thought of me that day.

"And yet I know — God knows how I know it — that you will not doubt the truth of what I ask you here to read, — the inclosed story of my unhappy acquaintance with the Keesner family, from the hour of my capture by the father and son, to my last words with the daughter before her death. No one who believed Keesner's story would have believed mine, had I insisted upon telling it in the court-room to save Babe's good name and my own ; there were other reasons why I could not tell it there and then.

"I put it in your hands now, to repeat to whom it may concern, or, if you think better, to keep as a trust from one woman to another, conveyed to you by me. For it is not so much *my* story as the story of Babe Keesner. My own story I have already told you — all but the end of it. It ends in my hopeless love for you.

"Yours,   JOHN TRISTRAM BODEWIN."

The story Josephine put carefully away for the time when it should be needed; but the letter, that was from Bodewin to herself alone, she kept always with her and read over and over the words in which he had called himself her lover. For a little while the joy of knowing as well as trusting that he was guiltless, and the more selfish joy of knowing herself beloved, helped her to bear the thought of his self-exile ; but soon she began to ask herself, each day with a sharper anxiety, how long that exile was to last. He had cut himself off from any hope of an answer to his letter. She knew not where he had hidden himself. She searched the papers for personal items from the remotest states and territories, and often her heart stood still at the glimpse of a name, and she feared to read the record of some lonely death, in the tragedy of which she had no part. She could not bring herself to show Bodewin's letter to her father, — his justification in that quarter she felt must come through some one else besides herself. Her life was full of duties and little cares that once had made her sufficiently happy, but now it seemed to her like the swollen November currents of the river that flowed past her window, — heavily circling and swooning back upon itself, yet borne helplessly onward.

It was about this time that Hillbury, on his way to New York, passed through Kansas City and stopped over one train for the sake of seeing Josephine. He sent her a note from his hotel on the morning of his arrival, asking her permission to call in the afternoon.

Josephine welcomed this opportunity as the one she had long waited for. Hillbury, of all others, was the one whom it most concerned to hear Babe Keesner's story — the one it most

behooved to cancel, as far as might be, the wrong
that had been done. She would not trust herself
with Bodewin's defence. Hillbury should have
the story as it had been given to her, in the words
of Bodewin's letter.

In the weeks since the trial, Hillbury had been
settling with himself in regard to Josephine. He
had come to a decision none the less impassioned
that it was tardy and deliberate. He loved her;
she was everything his wife should be, except
that in some ways she needed development. He
felt that he was singularly fitted for the happy
task of aiding that development. It was not in
Hillbury's nature to be humble, even in his love.
Why should he be, indeed? He was thoroughly
equipped and disciplined for exact work and
refined enjoyment, for appreciation or for judgment; why not for love? Each separate problem
of his life as it presented itself had been solved
by him in the most satisfactory manner. The
problem next in order was this beautiful young
woman, whose divine capacity for love he believed
in and longed to prove. He had watched the
progress of Bodewin's influence over her, at first
with curiosity but later with deepening unrest.
That influence was at an end now — it never

occurred to Hillbury that it could have survived the revelations of the trial. The juxtaposition of his own happiness, supposing happiness to be in store for him, with his friend's downfall was painful. But life was full of such pain, and the Nemesis that had overtaken Bodewin could not be appeased by any private renunciations of his own.

Did Hillbury but know it, his sorrow for his friend, and the trouble of mind it had cost him, together with his own share in Bodewin's condemnation, had done much to soften his pride of individuality, and to widen the gate of his well-guarded heart for love to creep in.

He was surprised to find how nervous he was becoming, while he waited for Josephine after sending up his card.

He watched her with keen pleasure as she came down the long room to meet him. Her beauty impressed him not more than her earnestness and entire unconsciousness of herself. She did not smile, but her face showed a gladness that was almost exaltation. Hillbury was not humble, but he was honest and clear-sighted. He could not take that unexpected deep joy in her face all to himself. He would have to come many times

to see her before he would have earned such a
beautiful look of greeting as that. It troubled
him to think of the unknown agencies that might
be swaying her life away from him, even during
these moments she was apparently giving to him.
She held a bulky letter, which she kept in her
hands, bending and crushing it, while she replied
to his inquiries about her father and the incidents
of their journey. For some time they talked of
indifferent things, carefully, on Hillbury's part,
avoiding any allusion to their common experi-
ences in the camp, or to any person connected
with them. It was Hillbury's intention to com-
mence again on a new basis with Josephine, ignoring as far as possible the unfortunate beginning
of their acquaintance — ignoring it until they had
become intimate enough to return to it from a
common point of view. Then they would talk of
it together, with assured sympathy, as of everything else in both of their lives that had been
remembered with pleasure or with pain. This
thought stealing into his mind was almost confus-
ing in its sweetness. There was a little silence.
Then Josephine bent towards him suddenly, her
hands clasped over the letter in her lap. " We
are thinking of the same thing, I know. Why

should we not speak of it?" she said, looking almost imploringly at Hillbury.

"Of what are you thinking?" he asked.

"Of the day when I saw you last. It seems to me I have thought of nothing else ever since." She did not see that her words were a blow to Hillbury. "I know," she went on, "how you must have suffered in doing what they made you do. It was worse for you almost than for your friend. For you believed he had sinned, and he knew that he had not."

She gave Hillbury a moment in which to speak, but he was silent.

"How strange it is," she continued, with an absent look of pain, "that the truth can be more cruelly false even than falsehood itself. The proofs were terrible, but it was the proofs that lied."

"How do you know that?" Hillbury asked, sternly. He felt as if he were now on his own defence.

"I have the true story here, in his own words — all those fatal omissions he was obliged to make; they are all explained here." She half opened the letter and held it towards Hillbury. "You are to read it," she urged, as he made no movement to take it. "You are the one oʈ all others who *must* read it."

Hillbury had recognized the handwriting. "If it is imperative that I should read it, why was it not addressed to me?"

"You forget there was a woman sacrificed with him," said Josephine coldly. "He has written in her defence, not in his own. But her cause and his are inextricable. In telling the truth about her, he shows how he himself has been misjudged."

"If there is anything he could have explained and did not, he has done a great wrong to others besides himself. A man owes the truth about himself to his friends at all times, and at certain times he owes it to all men. The trial was one of those occasions. Bodewin had no right to make omissions in his testimony. It is not the truth that is sometimes false, it is half the truth."

"But one may become involved through sympathy; through tenderness for others. He was bound by a promise to one who was dying, absolutely helpless and at his mercy."

It was unfortunate that these hastily chosen words of Josephine's called up a picture that was almost revolting to a man of Hillbury's stern probity and hatred of morbid sentiment. "I cannot imagine," he replied with deep-toned impatience, "any circumstances that should excuse a man for making an unconditional promise to conceal the truth, or a part of it."

"It is very possible that you cannot," said Josephine; "but that was not the question at the trial. The charges they made against him there are answered in this letter. Your own statements are answered. You owe it to yourself to read it." She offered him the letter again. She was hurt and disappointed by Hillbury's manner. She had expected that he would welcome Bodewin's explanations with unhesitating joy, but now it seemed as if he required some indorsement of the message itself. He took the letter and was about to put it away in his pocket-book, when Josephine interposed — "Oh, I cannot give it up to you; I must ask you to read it now. There are not many pages."

"I will return it to you, promptly," said Hillbury. "I would rather read it, if you please, when I am alone; you think me possibly more indifferent in this matter than I am."

It was impossible for Josephine to explain to Hillbury her feeling of passionate proprietorship in Bodewin's letter. It had come like a revelation, vouchsafed to her alone, out of the sad mystery of his fate. It was, to her simple imagination, the sole and sufficient proof of his innocence. She could not part with it, even for a day. Her pride deserted her in this dilemma; she looked helplessly at Hillbury, with tears in her eyes.

"Read it to me yourself," said Hillbury suddenly. "The words will come home to me more if I hear them uttered." He was not slow to comprehend her feeling. He suspected that he had made a dreary mistake — not the first one of that strange, unhappy summer. He wanted some sure proof of it. There could be none surer than to hear Josephine tell Bodewin's story in his own words.

She hesitated but a moment over the alternative. Then going to the window and seating herself between the heavy partings of the curtains, she began to read. At first her voice trembled and the pages of thin paper rustled slightly in her fingers. But soon she had lost herself in the story. Hillbury listened, but not with joy, for Bodewin's justification was his own sentence, and the final blow to the hope which had brought

him there. There was no mistaking the source
of this passion for justice that thrilled in the girl's
voice and made the blood in her cheek its witness. He saw the sweet delusion he had been
cherishing fade, and in its place he faced only the
cold, enduring peace of reparation for a wrong
unconsciously committed but no less cruel in its
consequences. He saw where he had failed in his
faith towards his friend. Failures or mistakes of
any kind were bitter things for Hillbury to acknowledge, but while he silently owned his shortcomings his habit of justice made him just, even
to himself. He did not accuse himself extravagantly. He had judged his friend only as he himself would have submitted to be judged by others.

When in the course of the narrative Josephine
came to the incident of the photograph, Hillbury
interrupted her. He did not understand Bodewin's allusion to his relations with Harkins
through the death of his sister. Josephine laid
down the letter and repeated to him the story of
Ellen Eustis's death.

"Was that the 'obligation' — the 'delicate personal obligation' that Bodewin suffered from?"
Hillbury exclaimed. "Poor fellow!" he added
gently. Bodewin's family pride and his sensitive-

ness through his sister would be sure to touch Hillbury far more nearly than any entanglement of sentiment, of gratitude, with a young woman of a class beneath him.

"How strange that he never told you that story!" Josephine murmured in the pause.

"May I add how strange that he told it to you!"

Josephine hung her head. "Before the trial," she explained falteringly, "he had told me many things about himself which our short acquaintance did not entitle me to know. But it came about through my presuming to ask him why he would not be my father's witness." Josephine felt how Hillbury would regard this statement. When the story had progressed as far as the scene on the porch, when Babe had submitted to have her eye treated, the reader laid the letter down and looked at Hillbury. "Is it not true," she said, "that proofs can lie? The only thing that can be trusted is character. A man thirty years old should have one. His friends, I think, should know what it is, and — forgive me — I think they should let no evidence, hardly the evidence of their senses, shake the faith that has once been given."

If Josephine was merciless, it was because Hillbury seemed to her so little moved.

"Spare me," he said in a low voice. "Yours was the better part; but it is possible that only a man can fully measure a man's temptations. And the effect of a thing *seen* is tremendous."

When Josephine had folded the letter, Hillbury rose and walked slowly towards the window where she sat. He still held his hat and gloves, and as he bent over her hand in farewell, he looked merely a perfectly dressed and irreproachable afternoon visitor taking his leave. Yet never in his life before had he been so deeply moved.

"What I have learned from you, Miss Newbold, makes it necessary that I should see John Bodewin as soon as possible. Can you tell where he is?"

"I have no idea," said Josephine.

"Does his letter give no clew?"

She shook her head. Her overwrought nerves were giving way and she could not trust herself to speak.

"Wherever he is," said Hillbury slowly, in his fine, sad accent, "I will find him, if he be living. When I see him I shall wish to say to him the thing that will be most comforting. He must be very sore —" He waited a moment. Josephine could not speak. "Your perceptions throughout have been so much truer than mine," he continued, — "Can you not give me the right words to say? There must be no more blundering. What shall I say that will be most sure to bring him back to us?"

"Oh," said Josephine, "if you find him, tell him I wish to see him; I have something to say to him myself."

"I will find him," Hillbury repeated, "and he will come."

As Hillbury walked back to his hotel he said to himself that the time had now come for testing the strength of those ideals to which he had pledged his manhood. Had not this visit ended better than his dream had planned? What happiness was there that a man should put before the truth and his own duty? And was his duty, then, so hard? To clear up a cruel misconception, to reverse an unjust judgment, to help a friend to the bliss that he must himself resign —

"I will find him, and he will come!" Many times in the days that followed Hillbury's visit, Josephine repeated these words to herself, and saw again his sad yet satisfied smile of prophecy. She lived upon the words until the promise was fulfilled.

CHAPTER XXVI.

THE DESERT STATION.

ONE day of the following summer an overland train, westward bound, left two of its passengers at a station on the desert plains, consisting of one frame house, a "dug-out," a section house, and a water-tank. It was not a meal station; no through train would stop there until the following day. A conveyance called a "jerky" would arrive in two hours' time from some obscure habitation of men in the desert, and continue thence to its next stopping-place, thirty miles away. But even this poor chance of rescue was not known to the sympathetic carload of passengers who were now abandoning two of their number to their fate.

The self-devoted ones were a woman in her first youth and a man not so young by several years. Both were interesting in appearance, and, as if to complete the contrast between herself and her surroundings, the girl was quietly but intelligently dressed in the height of the summer's fashion for young lady tourists, in the world where the fashions are a record of the seasons as they pass. While her companion was directing the porter who carried their hand-luggage, the young woman walked to the end of the short platform and stood there looking before her eagerly. In her happy eyes there was something like recognition of the scene, or a remembrance of some other scene which it vividly recalled. Strongly characterized as it was, there was indeed nothing singular in the view. Hundreds of miles of such country can be seen by the traveller west of the Missouri River. The sage-brush was turning gray with the long summer's deepening dust; the blue of the cloudless sky was darker than the sun-blanched plain; rising afar off where sky and desert meet, a range of peaks showed their snow-covered tops, like white sails on the horizon.

The young girl and her travelling companion stood side by side as the train moved off, watching the little colony, of which they had lately been a part, receding from their gaze down the lessening lines of the track. Two or three heads looked back at them from open windows. A

young man sitting on the steps of the rear car
waved his hat to them, with the compassion of
one who goes with the majority for the pathetic
minority left behind.

The two who were in the minority did not respond; they turned and smiled at each other.

"They are *sorry* for us!" said Josephine.

The man on the rear car was a mere speck in
the distance. Bodewin stooped and kissed her
for the look with which she said those words.

The noise of the train died away and they were
left standing alone on the heated boards of the
platform, enfolded in the stillness of the desert.
Gradually their stunned ears became accustomed
to the fainter range of sounds around them. The
ticket agent, who had partially satisfied his curiosity with regard to them, and returned to the
solitude of his official duties, could be heard rustling a newspaper and grating a chair across the
floor within. The hurried click, click of the telegraph machine asserted itself imperatively, like
the voice of the world they had left warning them
to come back. The wind from off the desert,
blowing in their faces, seemed to call to them
from that unknown region whither they were
venturing together. Josephine lifted her out-

stretched arms and welcomed it with a thrill of joy that was keen with the memory of pain. It was the wind of the high valley where she and Bodewin had ridden together — it was the plain's wind that had rattled the dusty lattices outside of the room where she lay, alone with her anguish, the evening after the trial.

Wind of the great Far West, soft, electric, and strong, blowing up through gates of the great mountain ranges, over miles of dry savannah, where its playmates are the roving bands of wild horses, and the dust of the trails which it weaves into spiral clouds and carries like banners before it! Wind of prophecy and of hope, of tireless energy and desire that life shall not satisfy. Who that has heard its call in the desert, or its whisper in the mountain valleys, can resist the longing to follow, to prove the hope, to test the prophecy!

* 9 7 8 3 3 3 7 3 9 8 6 6 8 *